Selected Short Stories of Premchand

Written by Premchand

Translated by Neeharika Singh Lodhi

Pharos Books

HB ISBN: 978-93-95862-53-0
ISBN: 978-93-95862-18-9
eISBN: 978-93-95862-28-8

©Publisher

Publisher: Pharos Books (P) Ltd.
Plot No.-63, 1ˢᵗ Floor, Main Mother Dairy Road
Pandav Nagar, East Delhi-110092
Phone: 011-40395855
WhatsApp: +91 9319228272
E-mail: bookspharos@gmail.com
Website: www.pharosbooks.in
Edition: 2025

Printed By: E.B. Print and Pack, Greater Noida

Selected Short Stories of Premchand
By Premchand

CONTENTS

"The world assumes that we are very happy with high mansions, fine carriages, servants and attendants, huge investments, and concubines. But he who is without the honour and strength of the soul can be anything but happy."

— Premchand

Introduction

Born in a village near Varanasi on July 31, 1880, Dhanpat Rai Srivastav popularly known by his pen name Premchand is one of India's greatest literary figures writing in Hindi and Urdu. He is famous to have written on subjects of social importance – exploitation and submission, greed and corruption, poverty and the rigid caste system. He is known to have written 14 novels, 300 short stories, several translations from English classics, innumerable essays and editorial pieces.

Premchand liked to portray a very real world. "I write for only one sake: To present a human truth, or to show a new angle of looking at common things," he wrote. Literature for him was a mirror of its age, definition, and scope and he believed that its contents just as much as its aims and objectives must change with time. He also urged writers to discard individual and personal concerns and, instead, speak in a collective voice taking upon themselves public and political roles.

It is this attribute of representing the world as it is which has made his literary works timeless. The nature and makeup of society, its people, the thoughts and emotions of people and their struggles that Premchand depicted almost a century ago still stir the readers today.

This collection of 12 short stories by Premchand is an attempt to bring to global readers the finest of Hindi literature in English. These stories depict the lives of people from different strata of society. By turns moving, witty, comical and tragic, many of his stories powerfully invoke the pastoral simplicity as well as its harsh realities, while others capture the hopes and anxieties in a city.

1. Eidgah

Eid has come after an entire month of fasting during Ramzaan. The day dawns with special brilliance. The trees seem greener. The fields look brighter. The sky is clear blue. And look at the sun! It seems to be sending out a special Eid greeting to the world through its soft, warm light. The village is abuzz with excitement.

People are getting ready to go to the Eidgah. There is a person who has just found out that his buttons are missing from his *kurta*[1]; he is running to his neighbours to get a needle and thread. There is another person whose shoes are new, so he is running to the oilman to put some oil onto them. Others are hurrying to feed the bullocks; it will be late afternoon by the time they return from the Eidgah. They have to travel almost three miles on foot and then meet and greet so many people. There is no way they can return home before noon.

The children are the happiest of them all. Some have kept just one fast, and that too for half a day; others haven't even done that, but their joy of going to the Eidgah is no less. Let the elderly keep the fasts; the boys are happy with their Eid! They have been waiting for this day for months. Now they are excited to reach the Eidgah. What do boys have to do with domestic matters? They don't care whether there is milk

---

1.   A long shirt

and sugar at home for the special *seviyaan*[2] that shall be made; they only know that they shall eat lots of *seviyaan* today. Little do they know why their poor father is running desperately towards Chaudhry Kayam Ali's house. Nor do they know that if the Chaudhry would turn his face away, their Eid will turn into a day of mourning. Their little pockets are filled with the treasures of Kuber, the God of Wealth. They take out their heap from the pockets and count every *paisa*[3]—again and again—and put it safely back.

Mehmood counts—one, two, ten, and twelve. He has twelve *paise*. Mohsin has one, two, three . . . eight, nine . . . fifteen. With these countless *paise*, they shall buy countless things— toys, sweets, bugles, balls and the list continues... The happiest of them all is Hamid— a thin, sickly-looking boy of four or five whose father died last year of cholera and whose mother dwindled slowly and she too passed away one day. No one knew what ailed her. She did not share her troubles, for there was no one to listen to her either. She suffered silently and when she could not take it anymore she quietly left the world. Now, Hamid sleeps in his grandmother Ameena's lap and he is no less happy. He thinks his father has gone away to earn lots of money and one day he will return home with bags full of money. And his mother has gone to Allah's house and she will return with lots of nice things for him. This is enough to make Hamid happy. Hope is a great thing, and there is nothing like the hope of a child. A child's imagination can make a mountain out of a grain.

Hamid is without shoes. On his head, he wears a tattered old cap whose gold lace has turned black with time. But he is happy. When his father will return with a bagful of money and

---

2.   Vermicelli pudding, a sweet delicacy prepared on Eid.
3.   A unit of money that is used in India.

his mother with new and fancy clothes, he will get everything his heart yearns for. Then he will see how Mehmood, Mohsin, Noore and Sammi can match his wealth.

Poor, unfortunate Ameena is sitting at her home and crying. It is Eid today and she does not have a grain in her house. Had her son, Abid, been alive, would Eid have come and gone like this? She is lost in the darkness of despair and hopelessness. Who had called for this good-for-nothing Eid? There is no use for it in this house! But Hamid has no such worries. He is unconcerned by such dark thoughts. There is light inside him and brightness in the world outside. Let misfortune come with all its strength; it will face defeat in front of Hamid's happy face.

Hamid enters the house and tells his grandmother not to worry. He shall be the first one to return home.

Ameena's heart is causing pain in her chest. The other boys are going with their fathers; Hamid has no one except Ameena. Can she let him go alone? What if he were to get lost in that crowd? No, no, how can she let him go alone? He is a little boy, after all, how can he walk six miles? He will get blisters on his feet. He doesn't even have shoes on his feet. If she were to go along, she could pick him up even now. But if she goes, who will cook the *seviyaan* at home? If she had enough money, she could have bought the necessary ingredients on her way back. But since she has no money she has to borrow all the things from her neighbours. It will take her hours to collect everything.

The other day she had stitched clothes for Fahiman for which she had been paid eight *annas*. She had been holding on to those eight *annas*[4] for this Eid. But yesterday, the milkman's wife had insisted on getting back the money due

4. A unit of money that is used in India.

to her. Poor Hamid, he needed to be given milk of two *paise* worth at least. But after paying for the milk, Ameena is left with only two *annas*—three *paise* in Hamid's pocket and five in Ameena's purse. That is all they have, and it is Eid today! Allah alone is their saviour. The washerwoman, the barber's wife, the sweeper's, the bangle-seller's—they will all come to greet her on the occasion of Eid. They will all expect their share of *seviyaan*, and they will not be happy with a little. How will poor Ameena escape from them? And why should she? Eid comes once a year. It is the time to offer alms to the poor and to take their blessings. May God keep her Hamid safe. These days too shall pass somehow.

2

The crowd left the village. And Hamid left with a group of boys. Sometimes they ran ahead and waited beneath a tree for the others to reach. Why were the elders walking so slowly? Hamid had wings on his feet. How could he tire so easily? They had approached the outskirts of the city. The orchards of the rich lined both sides of the road. They were covered by brick walls. Inside, there were trees filled with mangoes and litchis. Every now and then, a boy picked up a stone and targeted a mango. The gardener guarding the trees came out howling abuses. The boys had run off by then and were busy having a good laugh at fooling the gardener.

Tall buildings began to appear in the distance. There was the court, then the college, and then the clubhouse. How many boys must be studying in such a large college! They were not boys; they were men! They were grown-ups; with big moustaches, and yet were still studying! God only knew how long they would keep studying and what they would do with all their studies. There were a couple of big boys in Hamid's *madarsa*[5], good-for-nothing-types who ran away from work and were beaten every day. Surely, the same type of people must be ending up here. All sorts of magic were done at the Clubhouse. They said the skulls of dead men ran about and many great magical feats were performed, but no one was allowed to go inside. The *sahebs*[6] came here in the evenings to play—some had big moustaches and beards—and some came with their *memsahebs*[7] who played as well. If they tried handing a bat to our mothers: they won't even know how to hold one. They will take one swipe with it and fall over!

Mehmood said, 'My mother's hand will start shaking if she tries, I swear!'

Mohsin said, 'But she easily pounds kilos of wheat and you are saying her hand will tremble if she holds a bat! She draws countless pots of water from the well. My buffalo drinks at least five pots of water. Let one of these *mems* draw even one pot of water from a well, then they will know!'

Mehmood said, 'But our mothers don't run about and play.'

'They don't play,' Mohsin agreed, 'but just the other day when my cow got loose and ran into the Chaudhry's field, my mother ran so fast that even I couldn't keep pace with her!'

They kept walking. Shops selling sweetmeats began to appear beside the road. The shops were brightly decorated. Who could eat so many sweets? Each shop had kilos of sweets. One boy said, 'People say ghosts come at night and buy all the sweets. I heard from my father that a man appears at midnight, gets all the sweets weighed and pays real money for them.'

---

5. School run by Islamic organisation.
6. A courteous term used in the way "Mister" is used in the English language.
7. A courteous term meaning "Madam" usually refered to British/white females or female members of elite families in India.

Hamid found this hard to believe. He said, 'Where would the ghost get real money?'

Mohsin said, 'There is no shortage of money for ghosts. They can get into any treasure house they want. Not even iron doors stop them. They have lots of diamonds and jewels. If they are happy with someone, they shower them with jewels. They will be sitting here right beside you, and five minutes later they would have reached Calcutta.'

Hamid asked, 'These ghosts must be huge creatures?'

Mohsin answered, 'A single ghost can reach up to the sky while standing on the earth, his head touches the sky. But he can also fit into the pot.'

Hamid asked, 'How one can please them? If someone tells me the mantra to please a ghost, I would do it immediately.'

Mohsin said, 'I don't know the way how it is done, but Chaudhry *saheb* has many ghosts under his control. If anything is lost, Chaudhry *saheb* knows how to find it and also who took it. One day when Jumrati's calf was lost he could not find it for three days. But when he went to Chaudhry *saheb* he told him instantly that the calf is there in the animal shed, and there it was! The ghosts used to tell him the happenings of the whole world.'

Now Hamid knew how Chaudhry *saheb* had so much money and fame.

As they kept walking, they saw the Police Line. The constables were parading there. All night long they went round guarding otherwise there would be so many thefts. Mohsin countered, 'Actually the constables don't guard! But they do the theft themselves. They knew all the thieves and dacoits in the city. They tell the thieves to commit thefts in one neighbourhood while they themselves are in another neighbourhood and show off to the guard. And that is why these people have so much money. My uncle is a constable. He earns 20 rupees every month as a salary, then also he sends 50 rupees home every month. I had once asked him where he got so much money from. And he had laughed and said, 'Son, God gives it.' And then he said, 'I only take that much which won't tag me with a bad name and my job is also safe."

Hamid asked, 'if the theft is done by these people then why are they not caught?'

Mohsin felt sorry for such innocence and said, 'No one can catch them, you fool. It is they who catch people. But such acts are always punished by god. Ill-gotten gains are never fruitful. A few days ago, my uncle's house caught fire. He lost everything; not one vessel was spared. For several days he had to sleep under a tree. Then he took 100 rupees on loan from somewhere and bought pots and pans for the house.'

Hamid enquired if 100 was more than 50. 'Obviously. If 50 rupees fill one bag, then 100 rupees fill two bags,' he answered.

The houses were closely packed now. Crowds of people could be seen going towards the Eidgah. Each person was dressed in bright, colourful clothes. Some were travelling in horse-drawn wagons, others rode in motor cars. Everyone was bathed in the sweet scent of *ittr*[8]; everyone was filled with excitement. The small group of villagers, unaware of being in any way different from others, was lost in their own world of patience and contentment. For the children in that group, everything about the city was strange. Their eyes were glued to the things around them. Even the persistent sound of the horn could not break the spell. Hamid was so intent on looking around that he nearly got run over by a car.

---

8. Perfume

Suddenly Eidgah appeared in a dense cluster of tamarind trees giving shade, the floor of which was *pucca* covered with a mat. The lines of the faithful stretched far beyond the mat-covered floor. Those that were late placed themselves in the last rows. When there was no space in the front rows, even the rich and powerful went to the back. Everyone is alike in the eyes of Islam. The villagers too performed the ritual purification called *wuzoo* and took their place in the back row. Everything was so beautifully organized and arranged. Lakhs of heads bending down together and rising simultaneously. The mass of people bent, then sat with their knees folded behind them in perfect accord. This action was repeated several times. It looked as though lakhs of electric bulbs were switched on, then off, simultaneously. It was a wonderful sight to behold. It filled the onlooker's heart with pride, respect and joy. All these people here seemed to be strung together on a single thread of brotherhood.

3

Soon the prayer ended and people began to embrace each other. They attacked the shops selling sweets and toys. The villagers were in no way less excited than the children. Look, there! There is the swing! You can ride it for one *paisa*. One minute you feel you are going up to the sky, and the next minute you are falling to the ground. Up there is the spinning wheel with wooden elephants, horses, and camels hanging from the carousel. Twenty-five rounds can be enjoyed for one *paisa*. Mehmood, Mohsin, Noore and Sammi sit aside these wooden animals. Hamid remained standing some distance away. He had only three *paise*. He couldn't part away with one-third of his treasure for a few minutes of happiness.

The boys got off the carousel. Now, it was time to buy toys. A long line of toy shops could be seen where all types of toys could be found—the soldier and the village girl, the king and the lawyer, the water carrier and the washerwoman and the *sadhu*[9]. They were so beautiful and life-like, as though they would speak up at any moment. Ahmad bought a soldier, dressed in a khaki uniform, a red turban, and carrying a gun on his shoulder. It was like as if it had just come from a parade. Mohsin liked the water carrier. Its waist was bent under the weight of the water bag. With one hand it took hold of the water bag. It looked so jolly. In fact, it was singing a song. It looked as though any minute it would begin flowing water from its water bag. Noore had fallen in love with the lawyer whose face was shining with intelligence! It was embellished in a black gown on a long white coat and a gold watch hanging with a gold chain outside its front pocket. It clasped a legal file in one hand and looked as if it had been just out after arguing a case in a court of law. The toys would cost two *paise* each. Hamid had only three *paise*; he could not think of buying such expensive toys, which would break into small pieces if they were to fall from his hands. The tiniest splash of water would spoil their colour. What would Hamid do with such toys? What good were they for him?

Mohsin said, 'My water carrier will fetch water twice a day, morning and evening.'

Mehmood said, 'And my soldier will guard my home. If a thief comes, he will fire at him with his gun.'

Noore said, 'My lawyer will fight all my cases.'

Sammi said, 'My washerwoman will wash my clothes every day.'

---

9. Sage

Hamid did not think it was worth buying toys. After all, it was clay only which would break off the moment it would fall. On the other hand, he gleefully looked at the toys his friends had bought and wished to hold them in his hand for a moment. Heedlessly, he stretched out his hand for one but none of the boys offered them their new toy! Poor Hamid was left tempting. Now came the turn of sweet shops. Some bought *rewri*[10], another gulab jamun, yet another chose *sohan halwa*[11]. Everyone was enjoying the sweets—everyone except poor Hamid, who had only three *paise*. He looked on with hungry eyes.

Mohsin said, 'Hamid, come and have this *rewri*. Look its fragrance is so nice!'

Hamid was in a dilemma. He realised it was a wicked joke; Mohsin had never been giving. Still, he went up to Mohsin. Mohsin took a *rewri* and pretended as if he was giving it to Hamid. Hamid extended his hand to accept it, but Mohsin grabbed it back and put it in his own mouth. Mehmood, Noore and Sammi clapped their hands and laughed loudly. Poor Hamid felt very sad.

Mohsin said, 'This time I will surely give you one, I swear on Allah. Here, it is.'

Hamid answered, 'Keep it. Do you think I have no money?'

Sammi said, 'But what can you buy with only three *paise* in hand?'

Ahmad said, 'Come here and I will give you some gulab jamun; Mohsin is very indecent.'

---

10. A sweet
11. A sweet

Hamid said, 'Sweets are not healthy for us; the books say so.'

Mohsin said, 'I know in your heart you are thinking: 'I will eat them if I get one!' Why don't you spend your money?'

Mehmood said, 'I understand his motive. He will buy sweets after all our money is finished and will have them making us look on greedily.'

After the sweet shops, there were metal shops and shops selling fake jewellery. These were not a place to attract the boys. They went on forward, but Hamid stayed on at an iron shop. Here he saw several iron tongs on display. His grandmother did not have a tong. She unknowingly burnt her fingers whenever she took the chapatti off the fire. How happy she would become if he bought her a tong. Her fingers would never be burnt again. Also, there would be something of use in the house. Are toys any worth? Nothing, only a waste of money! They give only momentary happiness. After some time you don't even look at them. Or else they break by the time you reach home. The tong, on the other hand, is the most useful thing. It helps you take the chapattis off the pan and cook them directly over the fire. If someone comes to ask you for some live coals, you can pick them up from the fire. Poor Amma never has the time to go to the market to buy such things, nor does she have the money. She burns her hand every day.

Hamid's friends had gone ahead. They had stopped beside a sorbet stall and were drinking sorbet. Look, how mean they are! They bought so many sweets but did not give me even one! And then they ask me to play with them! Or do things for them! Now if they ask me to do anything, I will say— Go and eat more sweets and get sick and greedy. They will get sores on their tongues and get sick from eating out. They will steal money and get beaten up by their fathers. After all, books don't have false things written in them. I won't fall ill. Amma will see the tong and run to take it from my hand. She will give me thousands of blessings and show it to the neighbourhood women. Everyone in the village will talk about it. Everyone will say Hamid is a good boy: And these boys? Who will praise them, or give blessings? The blessings of your elders go straight to Allah and are heard instantly. I don't have money that is why Mohsin and Mehmood ill-treat me. I shall also ill-treat them now. Let them have their sweets and enjoy their toys. I shall not take their sweets, nor be scared by them. What if I am poor but I don't ask anything from anybody. Perhaps, one day my parents will return. That day I will ask these boys the number of toys they want from me. I shall give baskets full of toys to each one of them and show them how to behave with friends. It is not buying one-*paisa*-worth of *rewri* and teasing others while eating it all alone! They shall be laughing at my tongs. Let them!

He asked the shopkeeper, 'What is the cost of the tongs?'

The shopkeeper looked at him and finding no elder person with the boy said, 'For you it has no value.'

Hamid asked, 'Can it can be bought or not?'

'Why it could not be bought? Why else would I bring it here?'

'Then why don't you tell me: what is its cost?'

'It is six *paise*.'

Hamid's heart sank.

'Tell the last price.'

'The last price is five *paise*, take it or leave it.'

Hamid gathered all his courage and asked, 'Will you give it for three *paise*?'

Saying this, he walked with fear thinking that the shopkeeper might taunt and abuse him. But the man did nothing of that sort; instead he called Hamid back and handed him the tong. Hamid put the tong against his shoulder like a gun and began to march proudly toward his friends. He was all set to hear their disapprovals.

Mohsin laughed and said, 'Why have you bought a pair of tongs, stupid? What use is this to you?'

Hamid threw his tong on the ground and said, 'Try this with your water carrier and watch it breaking into little pieces.'

Mehmood said, 'But a tong isn't a toy!'

Hamid replied, 'Why not? Put it on your shoulder, it becomes a gun. Hold it in your hand and it becomes a fakir's instrument. I can if I want to use it like a musical instrument. With one touch, it can smash all your toys, whereas your toys can't do anything to my brave tong.

Sammi had bought a small tambourine. Fascinated by the power of the tong he said, 'Will you exchange it with my tambourine?'

Hamid looked at the tambourine with discontentment and said, 'My tong can break your tambourine's belly if it wants to. After all, it is nothing but a bit of animal skin pasted to make a dub-dub sound. A little quantity of water can destroy it. My brave tong can get through fire, water, storm and hail.'

Everyone was attracted by the tong, but they had finished all their money. Moreover, the shops were left far behind. It was already nine; the sun grew hotter and everyone now wanted to get back home soon. Even if they requested their father for more money, they wouldn't be allowed to buy tongs! Hamid is a clever little fellow! Now, they all knew why he kept his money safe for so long!

4

The boys were now divided into two camps. Mohsin, Mehmood, Noore and Sammi on one side and Hamid all alone on the other side. A tug of war began. Sammi changed his mind and joined Hamid. Although Mohsin, Mehmood and Noore were two-three years older than Hamid but they were nowhere close to matching Hamid's wits. He had the power of justice and the difference of opinion on his side. There was clay on one side and iron on the other. One is breakable, the other is not. If a lion were to come up right now, the water carrier would melt in fright, the soldier would throw his gun and move away, the lawyer would be so frightened that he would hide under his robe and lie down on the ground, but this tong—would bravely pounce on the lion and bulge its eyes out.

Mohsin tried his best and came out with the following argument: 'But howsoever hard it tries, it can't fill water.'

Hamid kept the tongs straight up and said, 'It will give one blow to the water carrier and he will go running to fetch water.'

Mohsin accepted defeat. But Mehmood came forward and said, 'What if your tong gets arrested, handcuffed and brought to the court? Finally, it will be at the lawyer's feet.'

Hamid was confused by this powerful disagreement. He said, 'But who will come to arrest my tong?'

Noore answered proudly, 'My soldier will do it, with his gun!'

Hamid made a face and said: 'How come this poor thing can arrest my lion-hearted tong? All right, let's have a wrestling match between them. After looking at my tong your soldier will run away, forget making an arrest!'

Mohsin came up with a new argument, 'Your tong will burn its face every day in the fire.'

He had thought Hamid would be quiet now. But that was not the case. Hamid was there with an instant answer, 'Only the courageous jump into the fire. Your soldiers, lawyers and water carriers can't do that. Only the bravest of the braves can jump into the fire.'

Mehmood tried one more time, 'The lawyer will rest on a table and chair, while your tong will lie on the kitchen floor.'

This argument reinvigorated Sammi and Noore. What a sensible thing to say! What else can a tong do except lie on the kitchen floor?

When Hamid could think of no suitable answer he said, 'My tong will not simply lie on the kitchen floor, but it will go and toss the lawyer off his chair and pack his law into his stomach!'

This was indeed a very good answer and had the desired effect on the audience, even though that bit about packing the law in the lawyer's stomach was senseless. The three warriors on the other side stood fixed. Law was something to be argued strongly, not something to be stuffed inside their stomachs. Still, the newness of the argument won them over. Hamid became the undisputed warrior in this battle of words. Mohsin, Mehmood, Noore and Sammi could not object and accepted the fact that his tong was the bravest of the brave.

Hamid got the respect that a winner receives from the defeated. They had spent three to four *annas*, on worthless items. But Hamid had proved his worth with just three *paise*. He was right: What are toys good for? They break. Hamid's tong will last forever.

Now the time for bargain began. Mohsin said, 'exchange your tong for some time with my water carrier.'

Mehmood and Noore offered their toys too.

Hamid had no objection to these peaceful offerings. The tong travelled from one pair of hands to another, and one by one the toys were given to Hamid. They were such beautiful toys!

Hamid comforted the subdued party. 'I was only ragging you. There is no comparison between the black iron tong and your pretty toys. But these words of comfort brought no satisfaction to Mohsin's friends.

Mohsin said, 'But we will not get any blessings for these toys.' Mehmood said, 'Forget blessings, we will get a beating instead. Amma will say: 'Could you find nothing except these clay toys in the entire fair?''

Hamid had to accept the fact that no one could be as pleased after seeing the toys as would his grandmother by the tong. He had only three *paise* and he did not regret the manner in which he spent them. Especially now that his tong had been declared the bravest of the braves and the undisputed king of toys.

Mehmood was hungry on the way. His father gave him bananas to eat. Hamid only got the chance to share that with Mehmood. The other boys could only look on. Such was the miraculous effect of the tong!

5

Excitement ran through the village by eleven o'clock: People had begun returning from the fair! Mohsin's younger sister ran to grab the water carrier from his hand. But as she jumped with joy, the water carrier fell to the ground and broke. This led to a bitter fight between the two. Both cried. Their mother heard the commotion, she scolded both of them with two slaps each.

Noore's lawyer found a more honourable end befitting a lawyer. The toy would not sit on the floor or in a wall niche. After all, due respect must be paid to his high position. Therefore, two nails were dug into the wall. A wooden plank was balanced on them with a paper carpet. And there sat the lawyer like a king sitting on his throne. Noore began to fan him with a handheld fan. After all, a lawyer is used to electric fans and cool khus mats in the court. He had to be fanned here too, lest the heat of the law may get into his brain! Noore fetched a weed fan and began to fan the lawyer. God knows whether it was the air current caused by the fanning or slight touch from the fan itself, but the lawyer fell to the ground from his high position. There was great mourning and finally, the broken bits of the lawyer were thrown on the garbage heap.

Mehmood's soldier was still left. He was given charge of guarding the village. But a soldier is no ordinary thing that can walk on his own feet. He would go about on a palanquin! A basket was brought. A few old red rags were spread inside it. The soldier was placed on them. Noore brought up the basket and began to go round and round his house. His two younger brothers smirked behind him, shouting, 'All those who sleep, stay awake, stay awake!' But Mehmood stumbled and fell. The basket fell down as well and the soldier came tumbling down and broke its leg. Mehmood discovered what a good doctor he could be! He stuck the leg back with a bit of gum from the gular tree but the moment the soldier got to his feet, the leg gave way again. When this operation proved unsuccessful, it was decided that the other leg must be broken too. Now, at least the soldier could sit in peace in one place; with one leg he could neither walk nor sit. From a soldier, it became a hermit. It would keep guard from one place only. Sometimes, it could pose as a god too. Its turban was scratched away so it could become whatever one wanted it to be. Sometimes it was used for measuring weight.

Now, let us know what happened to Hamid. Ameena had come running out when she heard his voice. She pulled him in her lap and began kissing him. Suddenly, she spotted the tong in his hands and stopped.

'Where did this come from?'

'I bought it.'

'For how much?'

'I gave three *paise* for it.'

Ameena wailed with disbelief. What a silly, innocent child! It is almost noon and he hasn't eaten or drank anything. And what has he bought? A pair of tongs!

'Could you find nothing else to buy in the entire fair?'

Hamid answered remorsefully, 'Your fingers get burnt when you take the chapattis off the wood fire; that's why I bought it.'

Instantly, the old lady's anger turned into love, not the sort of love that can be boldly expressed through words. It was a silent, wordless love, solid yet filled with the nectar of sweetness. She was surprised at the child's goodness, intelligence and self-control. He had thought of buying something for her when all the other children were buying sweets and toys! How had he controlled himself? Even there, at the fair, he was only thinking of his old grandmother! Ameena's heart overflowed with joy.

And then a strange thing happened. Stranger than Hamid's tong. Young Hamid turned into an older man and old Ameena turned into a child. She began to cry. She spread the corners of her scarf wide and continued blessing him as big drops of tears fell from her eyes. How could Hamid unravel this mystery?

2. Qazzaqi

Among all my childhood memories, the most enduring is that of Qazzaqi. Forty years have passed without seeing him but his picture is quite clear in my mind. In those days, I lived with my father in a *tehsil*[12] in Azamgarh district. Qazzaqi was of the Pasi caste. He was very cheerful, brave and a dynamic person. He used to bring the posts in the evening, stay overnight and then go back the next day with a bag full of letters to be delivered. The very same day he would return with the posts to be distributed.

I used to wait anxiously for him the whole day long. At four o'clock sharp, impatient for him to arrive, I would go on to the street and soon he would be seen running speedily, carrying a staff on his shoulder, ringing bells on it. He was a tall and well-built young man, with a tanned complexion. His body was so perfectly designed that even the most perfectionist art designers could not possibly find fault in it. His small moustache set off his well-shaped features to advantage. He would run even faster after he caught sight of me, the bells on his staff ringing more noisily—my own heart would beat even louder with joy at his arrival. I would dash across to meet him and, in a moment, Qazzaqi's shoulder would become my throne. That seat was the

---

12. A local unit of administrative division; township.

paradise of my naive aspiration. Perhaps even those who dwelt in paradise would not have experienced the same level of happiness that I did sitting atop the broad shoulders of Qazzaqi. The whole world would suddenly appear small and meaningless to me when he would sprint away, carrying me on his shoulders. I felt I was flying on a winged horse.

By the time he arrived at the post office, Qazzaqi would be sweating profusely, but resting was not in his habit. After depositing his bag he was out immediately with us in the field. Sometimes playing with us; at other times he would sing to us or tell us stories. He had a large repertoire of tales about burglary and stealing, murders and massacres, ghosts and spirits. I always listened to him with rapt attention, spellbound by the tales. The thieves and bandits of his stories were true heroes who stole from the wealthy to help the poor and the deprived. Rather than looking down upon them, I began to hold these men in high esteem.

2

One day, Qazzaqi was late. The sun had set but he was not to be seen. I felt rather lost and waited by the road, with wide eyes, but his familiar face was nowhere in sight. I strained my ears to hear the jingle of the bells on his staff but that cheerful resonance was not to be heard. As darkness overcame daylight, my hope began to fade. Every time someone came from that direction, I would ask expectantly, 'Is Qazzaqi on his way?' But they either did not listen to me or merely moved on with a nod.

Suddenly, I heard the familiar jingle. In the darkness that engulfed everything around me, I could perceive only ghosts—even the sweets stacked upon the mantle shelf in my mother's room were avoidable after dark. Despite the ghosts that cluttered my mind, I hurried in the direction of the sound. Yes! It was Qazzaqi. The moment I set eyes on him, my impatience turned to annoyance. At first, I began to hit him. Then I stood sulking at a little distance.

Qazzaqi chuckled and said, 'I have brought something for you but if you hit me, I will not give it to you.'

Gathering courage, I responded, 'Okay, go, don't give it—I do not want it.'

'If I show it to you, you will surely grab it with both hands.'

My annoyance melted into curiosity. 'All right, show it to me.'

'Come, climb on my shoulder—let us run away, it is rather late already—*Babuji*[13] must be worried.' I turned around and replied, 'First show me what you have brought!' Had Qazzaqi not been concerned with the fact that he had gotten delayed, had it been possible for him to stay back even a minute longer, he might have got the better of me. He showed me what he was holding close to his heart—it had an elongated head and eyes that shone brightly. I snatched it out of Qazzaqi's hands. It was a young deer. Ah! No one can measure the happiness I felt at that moment! I have passed many difficult examinations since then; I have been awarded high-ranking positions and enshrined with the title of Rai Bahadur. But the happiness experienced at that very moment still remains untouched. I took it in my arms, and enjoying its supple and fragile body, marched towards our house. It slipped from my mind that Qazzaqi had arrived late. 'From where did you get this?' I asked him.

---

13. A term of respect for one's father. 'Babu' can also be used as a term of respect for any respected elder or man.

'*Bhaiya*[14] there is a grove a little far away, where deers roam in large herds. I always wanted to give you a fawn if I could catch one. Today, I saw this fawn in the group. As I rushed towards it, the rest of the deers ran fast. This one also tried to escape but could not keep pace with the adults. I took hold of it. Due to this, I got late too. The two of us came to the post office chatting. *Babuji* could neither see me nor the fawn. His eyes were only looking for Qazzaqi. With rage, he asked, 'Why are you so late today? The postbag has been full since a long time! What should we do with it now as the post has already been sent out? Why are you so late? Answer me!'

It seemed that Qazzaqi had lost his voice.

Babuji continued criticizing him, 'In fact you do not want to do the work now. You are, after all, a mere low-caste. You are satisfied with two square meals a day, and it has turned your head, has it? Perhaps you will only understand when you are weak and dying of hunger.'

Qazzaqi did not utter a word.

Babuji only got angrier. He continued admonishing him. 'Put the postbag down and get back home. The swine has come in so late with the post. But does it affect you at all? No! You will be a manually employed labourer wherever you want to. But I will be held responsible for your shortcomings. I will be answerable.'

Qazzaqi looked as though he would burst into tears and said, '*Sarkar*[15], I will never be late again.'

'But why are you so late today? Answer me!'

---

14. Brother.
15. Sir; a man of the government.

Qazzaqi could not answer. I too seemed to have lost my voice. *Babuji* was very short-tempered. He had to work exceptionally hard. That is why he got furious so easily. I kept away from him and he too never expressed any love for me. He came home only twice during the day, for his meals, spending an hour each time. For the rest of the day he worked at the post office. He had sent in several applications for an assistant, which went unheard till date. The result is that even on holidays he had to work. Only mother could tackle his foul temper. But she could not come to the post office. Poor Qazzaqi was removed in the imperious manner credited to Nadir Shah of Afghanistan, while I stood and watched! His staff, *kamarband*[16] and turban were confiscated and he was issued stepping orders to be enforced with immediate effect. Ah! At that time I wished to be in possession of the gold-rich Lanka which I could bounteously offer Qazzaqi, so that he would never feel the slight pain of removal from service and father would know that Qazzaqi had not suffered a scrape. That would teach my father a lesson! Qazzaqi was just as proud of his *kamarband* as a soldier is of his sword. His hands shivered as he began to unfasten it. All the while, the root cause of his misfortunes, that tender living thing, was hidden away, seated ever so comfortably on my knees as though it were nestled in its mother's lap. As Qazzaqi began to leave, I too got up, following him step by step. When he reached the door to my house, he spoke, '*Bhaiya*, go inside. It is getting dark.' I stood without a word, trying exceptionally hard to fight back the flood of tears that threatened to break loose any moment. Again he came to me, '*Bhaiya*, I am not going far away. I will come again sometime and together we will

---

16. Belt

run with you on my shoulders. *Babuji* has fired me but surely he will not prevent me from playing with you! I will not leave you and go anywhere. *Bhaiya*, go inside and tell Amma that Qazzaqi is taking leave. Will she forgive his shortcomings?'

I ran into the house but instead of saying anything to my mother, I burst out crying. Mother came out of the kitchen and asked, 'What is the matter, son? Has somebody hit you? Has *Babuji* said something? Wait till your father gets home. Let me find out. He always seems to be beating you—don't cry, son, and don't ever go to him again!'

With an immense effort I managed to control myself and uttered, 'Qazzaqi . . .' my mother thought Qazzaqi had hit me. Oh! Let him come,' she threatened. 'I will ensure he is removed from service immediately. How dare he hit my darling boy? He is merely a *harkara*[17] after all? I will have his turban and staff confiscated right now.

Immediately, I corrected her. 'No, it was not Qazzaqi. But father has fired him. He confiscated his turban and his staff. Even his *kamarband* has been taken away.'

'Your father was wrong to do that. The poor fellow works quite sincerely. Why did he dismiss him?'

'Qazzaqi got late today. Having said that, I put the fawn down for my mother to see. There was no fear of his running away within the house. My mother had not set eyes on it yet. The moment she did so, she became utterly concerned. She came forward and caught hold of my hand, fearing that the petrified animal would bite me! On the one hand, I was crying hysterically and on the other, I burst out laughing at her confusion.

---

17. Messenger

'Oh! This is the young one of a deer! From where did you get it?'

I narrated the entire episode of the fawn and its dreadful consequences from beginning to end. 'Mother, this fawn runs so fast that no one could have ever caught it. It can run as fast as the wind. Qazzaqi chased it for about four or five hours—only then did he manage to catch hold of it for me. Mother, nobody in the whole world can run as fast as Qazzaqi. That is why he got late—but *Babuji* dismissed the poor man and took away his *kamarband*, turban and staff. What will he do now? He will go hungry and die.'

'Where is Qazzaqi?' asked mother. 'Bring him to me.'

'He is waiting outside. He says, 'Request Ammaji to forgive my shortcomings.' All this while, mother had been making fun of what I had been saying. Perhaps she thought that *Babuji* had merely reprimanded Qazzaqi. It is only on hearing my last statement, she realized that *Babuji* had actually dismissed Qazzaqi from service. She went out immediately and began calling out, 'Qazzaqi . . . Qazzaqi . . .' but there was no sign of him. I called out to him again and again; I wept and called out his name but in vain.

I had my dinner. Children do not go hungry even when they are crestfallen, especially if *rabri* is placed before them. However, as I lay in bed, thoughts whirled in my head till late into the night— if I were in possession of a hundred thousand rupees, I would give it to Qazzaqi and tell him to say nothing to *Babuji*. The poor man was going to die of hunger. Would he come tomorrow? Why should he come now? But he said he would come again. I would get him to eat with me tomorrow. I fell asleep building such castles in the air.

3

I spent the next day looking after the fawn. First I gave it a name—Munnoo. Then I introduced it to my friends and classmates. In just a day it become so attached to me that it followed me everywhere. In a short span of time it became the central thing in my life. In the palace of my dreams that I intended to build at some point in the future, there would be a separate room for the fawn. I also intended to have a bed and phaeton for it.

By the time it was evening, however, every thought was abandoned and I stood on the road waiting for Qazzaqi to come. All logic was against his arrival but there was something which made me believe that he would come. All of a sudden I thought that he could be dying somewhere with lack of food. I went inside. Mother was lighting evening lamps. I took out some flour in a basket quietly and dropping some along the way, I ran out and reached the road. I had hardly completed doing so when I saw Qazzaqi approaching me. He carried a staff; on his waist he wore a *kamarband* and on his head there was a turban. I ran over to him and threw my arms around his waist and, in undisguised surprise, I inquired, 'From where did you get the *kamarband* and the staff, Qazzaqi?' He took me in his arms and, raising me on to his shoulders, he replied, 'What was the use of that *kamarband, bhaiya*? It was the *kamarband* of subjugation. This one is of my own making. At first I was the employee of the government but now I am your servant!'

As he was saying this, his eyes went to the flour basket kept right there. 'What is this flour for, *bhaiya*?' he asked. Feeling a little low, I replied, 'I have brought it for you. You must be hungry. What did you eat today?' I was not able to see

Qazzaqi's eyes as I was on his shoulders, but positively, from the tone of his voice, I could judge that he was drowned. '*Bhaiya*, how can the chapatti be eaten? There is neither salt nor dal and no ghee either.'

I felt thoroughly embarrassed. He was right. How could anyone eat dry *chapatis*? But how could I arrange for salt, dal and ghee? Now, my mother would be in the kitchen. With immense good fortune, I had managed to bring the flour. (Being ignorant of the truth that my theft had already been discovered by the trail of flour on the floor.) How could I arrange these three things now? My mother would never hand them over to me even if I requested her. She made me wait for hours for every *paisa* that I asked for—how could she give me all these items? Instantly it struck me that I had several *annas* and *paise* in my school bag. As a child, I would gather small amounts of money—I do not know when I left this habit. Had the practice been still there, perhaps I wouldn't be so yearning for funds as I am today. *Babuji* never expressed any liking for me but he made sure to keep my pockets warm, may be because he was so busy all the time or because he wanted to keep himself away from me; he must have realised that this was the easiest method. If he ever wanted to refuse, he feared the risk of my crying or throwing tantrums. He presumed the consequences and avoided the outcome. Mother's temperament was quite the opposite. She never feared my crabbiness. In fact, she could get through her household chores amidst my tantrums. A man can lie in bed all day long and listen to someone crying but any harsh jarring tone can be disturbing while one is busy making mathematical calculations. Mother loved me very much but the moment anybody made a reference to money, her humour underwent a drastic change. There were no books in my bag but there were certain forms of the post office which I kept folded like the books. I pondered whether the money I had would be sufficient for the purchase of dal, salt and ghee. After all, I could not grasp all of it in my fist. Having thought about all this, I said to Qazzaqi, 'If you put me down, I will bring you some dal and salt. But you have to promise me to visit every day?'

'*Bhaiya*, how could I refuse to come if you feed me every day?'

Promptly I responded, 'I will arrange your food every day.'

'Then I will come to visit you every day.'

I got down and ran into the house to bring the money I had. Were I in hold of the Kohinoor diamond, I would have offered it to Qazzaqi without any hesitation in lieu of his daily visits.

With a great deal of surprise, Qazzaqi asked me, 'Where did you get so much money from, *bhaiya*?'

With pride, I responded, 'It is mine!'

'Your mother will beat you. She will hold me responsible for having tricked you and bringing it to me. *Bhaiya*, you can have some sweets with this money and put the flour back in the urn. I will not die of hunger. I will use my hands—I can work. How can I die of hunger?'

Over and over again I told him that the money was mine and that he could take it, but he refused. He strolled around with me for a long time; he sang songs for me, then dropped me home and went away. He also left behind the flour basket at the door.

Scarcely had I stepped into the house when my mother yelled at me, 'you thief, where have you taken the flour? Now you are learning to steal as well! To whom have you given the flour? Tell me at once or I will skin you alive!'

I was in a predicament as I heard my mother's angry words. It was serious trouble. Mother was like a lioness when she was angry. I mumbled, 'I have not given it to anybody.'

'Haven't you taken out the flour? Look how much flour lies sprinkled all over the courtyard.' However much she scolded me or rebuked me, I was not in a position to utter a word. The confusion that lay in front of me was so serious that I fell down by its pull. I could not even gather up the courage to ask her why she was so furious. The basket was outside the door but I did not dare to bring it in either. In other words, I had lost all courage to act—my legs were heavy and I could not move. Suddenly Qazzaqi called out, '*Bahuji*, the flour is lying at the door. *Bhaiya* had taken it to give it to me.'

My mother immediately went to the door. She did not observe *purdah*[18] for Qazzaqi. Whether or not she talked to him I do not know, but she went inside with the empty basket. Then she got into the storeroom, took out something from the purse and walked back to the door. I saw that her fist was closed. I could not wait any more, just standing there. I went after my mother. She called him several times but Qazzaqi was already gone. Gathering all the courage, I offered to go and look for him but, bolting the door, my mother asked, 'Where will you look for him in the dark? He was here just now. I asked him to stay till I came back. I wonder where he went so quickly! He is a very modest person. He was not willing to take the flour but I insisted and poured it in his scarf. I feel very sorry for him. I wonder whether the poor fellow has any food to eat. I had brought some money for him. I wonder where he could have gone.'

---

18. The practice in certain Muslim and Hindu societies of screening women from men or strangers by using a veil.

Now, I gathered up some more courage. I told the entire story of my theft. When parents interact with children by becoming children themselves, they are able to exert greater influence. They can deliver better instructions too.

'Why didn't you ask me? Wouldn't I have given Qazzaqi some flour?' asked mother.

I made no reply but thought instead, 'Right now you are filled with pity for Qazzaqi, so you will give him whatever you feel. Had I requested some charity, you would have certainly beaten me up instead.' However, I was now relieved that Qazzaqi would not go hungry; that mother would give him something to eat every day and that he would take me out for a jaunt every day.

I spent the following day playing with Munnoo. In the evening I went out and stood by the road. It grew dark but Qazzaqi was not to be seen anywhere. Silence engulfed the roadside and soon the lamps were lit but Qazzaqi did not come. I returned home crying. 'Why are you crying, son?' asked mother. 'Didn't Qazzaqi come by?'

I began to cry even more loudly. Mother held me close. I got the feeling that she too was moved to tears. 'Be quiet, son. Tomorrow I will send a *harkara* to look for Qazzaqi,' she said. I fell asleep crying softly to myself.

The following morning, as soon as I awoke, I said to mother, 'Send for Qazzaqi!'

'I have sent someone already, son. Qazzaqi should be on his way,' replied mother.

Happy once again, I began to play. I was very certain that my mother would do as she had promised. She had dispatched a *harkara* early in the morning. At about ten o'clock when I returned home with Munnoo, I learnt that Qazzaqi had not been found in his house. Instead, his wife had been weeping because apparently he had not returned home. She feared that he had run away.

It is hard to understand what soft-hearted children have; they are unable to put down their feelings in words. Mostly, they are also not able to judge exactly what it is that is troubling them; which spike it is that is piercing their hearts, or what it is that which makes them cry every now and then. Why is it that they sit by themselves, downcasted and unable to take heed in playing? I was in such a state. I would keep going in and out of the house and then coming out again to stand by the roadside. My eyes looked for Qazzaqi. Where had he disappeared? Had he run away somewhere?

That evening, I kept standing by the road looking rather lost. Suddenly, I saw Qazzaqi out there in the lanes. Yes, it was Qazzaqi. I ran, calling out his name towards him as I used to, but found no sight of him anywhere. I wondered where had he vanished. I looked here and there from one end of the lane to the other, but couldn't even catch his smell.

I went home and narrated this to my mother. I sensed that my experience had moved her to intrusion.

Qazzaqi could not be seen anywhere for the next two or three days. Soon, he too began to slip from my mind. Little children are very likely to show a great deal of fondness at one point in time but they are also likely to forget things easily at another. They may be exceptionally fond of a particular toy but they may also smash it as easily once they get tired of it.

One afternoon, about ten or twelve days later, *Babuji* was having his lunch. I was engaged in trying brass anklets on Munnu's feet. A woman covered in a *purdah* walked in and stood in the courtyard. Her clothes were dirty and shabby but she was fair and charming.

'*Bhaiya*, where is your wife?' she asked.

I walked up and enquired, 'Who are you? What are you selling?'

'I am selling nothing. I have got some lotus seeds for you. *Bhaiya*, you love lotus seeds, isn't it?' I looked ardently at the cloth bundle she held in her hands and interrogated, 'From where have you brought me these? Can I look into them?'

'Your *harkara* has sent them for you, son,' she replied.

I was overwhelmed with joy and asked her, 'Qazzaqi?'

The woman shook her head and began to open the bundle. Just then mother came out of the kitchen; the woman immediately bent down and touched her feet in respect. 'Are you Qazzaqi's wife?' asked mother.

The woman bowed her head in response.

'What does Qazzaqi do for a living these days?' asked mother.

The woman began to cry and replied, '*Bahuji*, since the day he returned from your place with the flour, he has been ill. He constantly calls out for *bhaiya*. All his affection is reserved for *bhaiya*. He calls out '*Bhaiya, bhaiya*' every now and then and dashes towards the door. I wonder what has gone wrong with him. Sister, one day he disappeared from the house without saying a word to me; he hid in a lane and kept watching *bhaiya* for a long time. When *bhaiya* spotted him, he slipped away quietly. He is ashamed to come in front of you.'

'Didn't I tell you that, mother?' I interrupted.

'Do you have anything to eat at home?'

'Yes, sister, by your blessings, we are not hard-pressed for food. Today he woke up and walked up to the pond. I kept asking him not to go out as he was sure to catch a chill in the wind. But he did not listen to me. His legs tremble with weakness now. He waded into the pond and plucked out these lotus seeds for you and asked me to give them to you. *Bhaiya* is very fond of lotus seeds, he said. He asked me to inquire after you.'

I took out the lotus seeds from her bundle and happily began to munch on them. My mother stared at me but I pretended not to see her. I didn't have the patience to wait.

'Tell him that we are all fine,' said mother, and I added, 'Also tell him that I have called him. If he does not turn up, I will never talk to him again, I swear.'

By this time *Babuji* had finished his lunch and came out. Wiping his hands and his face with a towel, he conveyed his message, 'And do convey to him that *Babuji* has restored his services. He must come as soon as possible or *Babuji* will be forced to employ someone else.'

The woman took up the cloth and left. Mother called her out but she did not reply. Possibly mother ought to give her some flour and pulses.

'Have you really restored him to service?' asked mother.

'Of course! I would not send for him in jest. I had sent the report for his restoration to the service on the fifth day itself.'

'That is wonderful.'

'This is the only antidote to his ailment.'

4

When I woke up early the following morning, I saw Qazzaqi walking toward us supporting himself with a stick. He had grown frail and weak. He was looking so aged in such a short span of time—as though a verdant tree had withered and become stump-like. I ran towards him and hugged his waist. He kissed my cheeks and tried to lift me up so that he could put me onto his shoulders but he wasn't able to do it. Instead, he went down on his fours and I jumped onto his back. In this way, Qazzaqi crawled to the post office, with me riding piggyback. At that time, I could not contain my happiness but Qazzaqi might have been happier than I was.

'Qazzaqi, your service has been restored. Make sure you are never late again!'

Qazzaqi fell at my father's feet, crying uncontrollably.

It was not in my destiny to enjoy the pleasure of the company of both Qazzaqi and Munnoo simultaneously. When Munnoo was there, Qazzaqi moved out of my life, and when Qazzaqi came back to me, Munnoo slipped out of my hands. I miss Munnoo deeply to this day. Munnoo used to eat with me in my plate; he ate nothing until I was there with him to eat. He liked boiled rice very much; but, only when ghee was liberally put on it did he feel satisfied. Also he used to sleep and wake up with me. He was so particular about cleanliness that he always went outside to the nearby field, to relieve himself. The stray dogs were also kept away by him and it was not possible for any to enter the house. The moment he saw one, he would chase it out instantly, even if it meant leaving his meal.

Having left Qazzaqi at his work in the post office, I returned home for my meal; Munnoo too joined me. Hardly had I eaten two or three morsels when we spotted a large, ferocious-looking stray dog in the courtyard. Immediately, Munnoo stopped eating and chased it out. Dogs can become as meek as mice when they are on unfamiliar ground. The ferocious-looking animal took to his heels the moment he saw Munnoo. Munnoo ought to have returned after completing his mission. But this particular dog was the angel of Munnoo's death. Not content with merely chasing him out of the compound, Munnoo pursued him into the field nearby. Perhaps Munnoo did not realize that there, on neutral ground, he could never have the upper hand—he could never get the better of the fierce animal. Munnoo and the ferocious-looking dog were now on a level platform. He had chased so many dogs out of our compound that perhaps he had begun to overestimate his own power. He had also forgotten perhaps that outside the household limits, the owner's rights too go a long way in providing shelter and security. Hardly had the two animals reached the field when the dog turned around and attacked Munnoo, snapping at his neck with his sturdy canine jaws. Poor Munnoo was not even able to utter a sigh. I ran out upon hearing the commotion made by the neighbours, but it was too late. Munnoo lay dead and the ferocious-looking dog was nowhere to be seen.

3. Gulli-Danda[19]

Our English-speaking friends might disagree, but it is a fact that gulli-danda is the king of sports. Whenever I see boys playing gulli-danda I am overjoyed and feel like joining them. This is a game where there is no need for a lawn, or a court, or a net, or a bat. Just cut a bough of a tree, make a gulli and even if two people join in, you can begin the game.

The problem with foreign games is that their gears are very costly. You have to spend at least a hundred rupee note to get yourself qualified as a player. But for gulli-danda you have to spend nothing, and yet all the fun is yours. But we are so much in love with English things that interest in our own games has been lost. In the schools too, they charge three to four rupees every year as sports fees. But no one thinks of promoting Indian games that can be played without spending anything. The English games are meant for those who have money. Why force these on the poor? True, that a shot of gulli-danda can smash your eye. But so can a cricket ball— it can smash your head, or damage your ligament, or break your leg. If I still carry a scar on my forehead from gulli-danda, many of my friends have exchanged their bats for crutches. Well, it all depends on your interest. For me it is gulli-danda, and some of my sweetest memories are associated with this game.

---

19. A game in which a large stick is used to hit a small oval-shaped piece of wood.

Coming out early in the morning, climbing a tree to cut a few branches, chiselling out the gullis and dandas, the excitement and involvement, that crowd of players, that batting and fielding, those fights, that innocence in which all the differences between the upper-caste and untouchables, between the rich and the poor disappeared, where there was no room for pretence, or display of one's wealth, or pride– all this would be forgotten. The family is being angry, father is showing his anger on food, mother, who cannot think beyond the household, is of the view that my bare future is rocking like a sinking boat. And here I am busy sending my opponents on a gulli chase, not caring to wash or eat. A gulli is so small, but it is packed with the sweetness of all the sweets and pleasures of all the spectacles of the world.

Among my playmates was a boy named Gaya. He was elder to me by two-three years— thin, tall, long and thin fingers, quickness like that of a monkey, and so was his irritability. The gulli might be of any shape, but he pounced upon it like a lizard at an insect. I didn't know whether his parents were alive, or where he lived or what he ate but he was a champion player of our gulli-danda club. The team for which he played was sure to win. On seeing him come we would dash towards him and urge him to join our team.

One day I and Gaya were playing. He was batting and I was fielding. It is so strange that we enjoy batting the whole day but get tired of fielding in a minute. I tried all the tricks to wriggle out, everything that could work in such a situation, even tricks that are outside the rule book, but Gaya was not willing to let me go without completing his batting.

When all my requests failed I deserted the field and ran toward home. Gaya ran after and caught me, and wielding the danda, said, 'Go only after I have completed my batting. You were enjoying while I was fielding, and now you are running away when it is my turn to bat.'

'If you keep batting the whole day, should I keep fielding?'

'Yes. You'll have to go on for the whole day.'

'And without food and water?'

'Yes, you can't go until I have had my turn.'

'Am I your slave?'

'Yes, you are.'

'I'm going home. Let me see how you will stop me.'

'How can you go home? It's no joke. You have had your turn. Now, I must have mine.'

'Ok, yesterday I had given you a guava to eat. Give it back to me.'

'That's gone into my tummy.'

'Take it out. Why did you eat it?'

'I ate it because you gave it. I didn't ask for it.'

'I won't field until you return my guava.'

I thought justice was on my side. I must have given him that guava out of some selfish motive. Who acts without self-interest? People even do charity out of selfishness. So if Gaya had eaten my guava he had no right to ask me to field. People even forget a murder after being bribed and this fellow has eaten my guava without wanting to give anything in return? I had bought five guavas for one paisa; which even Gaya's father won't be able to afford. He was being unjust through and through.

Gaya drew me towards himself and said, 'I want my turn. I don't care about your guava or whatever!'

I had justice on my side and he was bent upon being unjust. I wanted to run away but he wouldn't let me go. I swore at him and he replied with a murkier word, and even slapped me. I bit him with my teeth. He hit me with the danda. I started crying. Gaya couldn't hit back against this weapon of mine and ran. I wiped my tears quickly and forgot the pain and went home laughing. I, the son of a police constable was beaten up by a low caste boy! I felt dishonoured but I didn't talk about it to anyone at home.

2

Soon my father was transferred. I was so excited at the idea of exploring a new place that I felt no remorse about leaving my friends. Father was not happy. Here the earnings were good. Mother was also not happy because everything was economical here, and she had become well acquainted with the neighbourhood women. But I was very happy. I was boasting to my friends— there the houses are well-guarded, they are skyscrapers, the teachers there in English medium do not have the right to beat a student, they might end up behind the bars for beating a child. The wide-open eyes and wonder-struck faces of my friends were telling me how high I had risen in their esteem. The ability the children have to turn unreal into the real can't be put into words by us who can convert truth into falsehood. The poor fellows were feeling jealous of me and looked as if they are saying: You are blessed, brother. Go. We have to live and die here only as this is our fate.

After twenty long years, I became an engineer. I was posted in the same town for inspection and lived in the post office bungalow. My very presence in that place surrounded me with the sweet memories of my childhood. I took up my stick and came out to walk by the town. My eyes searched eagerly, like a thirsty traveller, for my childhood haunts, but here there was nothing similar leaving apart the name of the town. In place of wastelands, there were pucca houses now. There was a beautiful park in place of the banyan tree. The place had been renovated. Had I not remembered the name and area, I wouldn't have identified it. The unmatched memories of my childhood were opening their arms to welcome my old friends, but things had changed. I wanted to hide the place in my heart and weep, and complain that it had forgotten me. I died to see its old face.

Suddenly I saw two-three boys playing gulli-danda in an open area. It slipped off my mind for a second that I was: a big officer, with my officership, power and authority in full display.

I went closer to them and enquired, 'Son, does anyone by the name of Gaya lives here?'

One of the boys answered, somewhat elated, 'Gaya? Gaya, the chamar[20]?'

I said, 'Yes, yes, the same. If there's anyone called Gaya, he would be the same.'

'Yes, there is.'

'Can you call him?'

The boy went and soon I saw him returning back with a tall, black giant kind of a man. I recognized him from a distance and wanted to take him in my arms but stopped for some reason. I said, 'Gaya, do you recognise me?'

Gaya bowed down to salute me 'Yes, my lord. Why wouldn't I? How have you been?'

---

20. A member of Hindu caste whose traditional caste occupation is leatherworking. Considered a low-caste as per the caste heirarchy in the Hindu social system.

'Oh! I am ok. And you?'

'I'm deputy sahib's syce.'

'What about Mattai, Durga and Mohan? Do you have any news about them?'

'Mattai's no more. Durga and Mohan have become postmen. And you?'

'I'm the district engineer.'

'Sarkar, you were always very intelligent.'

'Do you play gulli-danda still, sometimes?'

Gaya looked at me with surprise, 'How can I play, sarkar? I get no time off.'

'Come, let's play today. You bat. I'll field. I owe you a turn. Take it today.'

Gaya agreed only after great spur. He was a mere low-wage labourer. And, I was a significant officer. We were mismatched. He was feeling embarrassed. And me too. Not because I was playing against Gaya but because I felt that people would look at this as some sort of display and gather in a big crowd. I won't enjoy playing with a mass watching us, but I couldn't forego the temptation to play either. We decided to go and play in a remote and lonely place where there would be no one to watch us and we would relive the sweet memories of our childhood. I and Gaya came to the post-office bungalow and both of us drove to an open spot in the motor. We brought an axe too. I was very serious about it but Gaya was still taking it as fun. There was no sign of excitement or pleasure on his face. Perhaps he was lost in thinking about the difference which existed between us now.

I asked, 'Gaya, tell me honestly, did you ever think of me?'

Gaya replied, somewhat shying, 'How should I remember you, hazoor[21]? I'm worth nothing. It was my good luck to play with you for a few days. Otherwise, where do I count?'

I said, disheartened a bit, 'But I always have you in my mind. Your danda, with which you hit me hard. Don't you remember it?'

'That was out of childishness. Don't remind me of that, sarkar.'

'What! That's the best thing I remember of my childhood. The pleasure that I get remembering that incident is nowhere to be found; neither in the respect I get, nor in the money I have. There was something in that which is still sweet.'

Talking like this, we drove nearly three miles away from the town. There was silence all around. Towards the west was the marshland spreading for miles across, where we sometimes came to collect lotus flowers and we would tie them onto our ears like earrings. The evening of the month of June, saturated in ruby light. I quickly went up to a tree and came down after cutting a branch. And a gulli and danda were ready in no time.

The game started. I set the gulli on the small boat-shaped hole, the starting point, and struck it with the danda. The gulli went right in front of Gaya. He put his hands joined in the manner to catch a fish, but the gulli fell just at his back. It was the same old Gaya in whose palms the gulli would lie as if out of its own will. Wherever Gaya might be standing to the right or to the left, the gullis would just go into his hands, as if he had pulled them. The new gulli, the old gulli, the big gulli, the small gulli, the sharply tapered gulli, the untapered gulli —whatever may be the shape or size of the

---

21. Sir

gulli, all would go straight to his side, as if drawn by some magnetic power. But today the gulli seemed to have no love for him. After that, I sent him on a gulli chase. All the rules of the game were broken by me. I substituted cheating for lack of my practice. I continued playing even when I had missed hitting the gulli; although by the rules, it should have been Gaya's turn to bat. Whenever I failed to push the gulli at a distance, I ran to pick it up and started again. Gaya was observing all these wrongdoings, but he kept quiet as if he did not remember the rules at all. His target was so perfect that the gulli would always hit the danda with a clatter. The gulli's only aim after release from his hand was to strike the danda. But today it just couldn't hit the danda. It went either left or right or fell short, or went across.

After he had fielded for half an hour, the gulli hit the danda. But I cheated saying it had gone past missing it narrowly.

Gaya didn't protest.

'It might have missed.'

'Had it hit, I won't have denied it.'

'No, bhaiya, why should you lie?'

During our childhood days, he wouldn't have spared my life had I cheated like this. He would have caught me by the neck, but today I was cheating so openly. This jackass! He had forgotten everything.

Suddenly the gulli hit the danda like a bullet. Against this clear proof, I couldn't cheat, yet once again I thought of changing the truth into falsehood. What would I lose? If he agreed it would be great but if he didn't there was no harm in fielding for a while. I'll wriggle out appealing for bad light. Who would come again to the field?

Gaya shouted in a victorious mood, 'It has hit! It has hit! With a clatter.'

I pretended. 'Did you see it hit? I didn't.'

'It made a clattering sound, sarkar.'

'It might have hit a brick.'

How such a sentence came out of my mouth, surprised even me. To turn this truth into prevarication was like calling the day night. Both of us had seen the gulli hit the danda, yet Gaya accepted my version.

'Yes, it must have hit a brick. Had it hit the danda it wouldn't have made such a clattering sound?'

I began to bat again. But after such obvious cheating I began to pity Gaya's innocence. So when the gulli hit the danda a third time I accepted to field, out of kindness.

Gaya said, 'Now it's getting dark, bhaiya, we will play tomorrow.'

I gave a moment thought: Tomorrow there would be too much time and for how long I will have to field in front of him, only God knows that. It is better to play today itself.

'No, no. There's too much light. You take your turn.'

'The gulli won't be visible to us.'

'Don't worry.'

Gaya started to play. But he was dreadfully out of practice. He tried to strike the gulli twice but failed every time. His chance was over in less than a minute. The poor guy had fielded for an hour but had lost his turn just in one minute. I tried to be liberal.

'You can take one more chance. You have missed your very first shot,' I said.

'No, bhaiya, it's dark already.'

'You're out of practice. Don't you play now?'

'There's no time, bhaiya.'

Soon it was time to light the lamps. We both got inside the car and drove back to the town. As he was parting away, Gaya said to me, 'Tomorrow there'll be a match here. All the old players would come. Would you come? They'll come when you are free.'

I consented and was present there in the evening to watch the match. There were ten players in all. Some of them were my childhood friends. Most of them were young players, whom I did not know. The match started. I was watching sitting inside my car. Today I was surprised to see Gaya's skill. The gulli flew into the sky as he struck it. There was no trace of yesterday's hesitation, unwillingness or lack of interest. What was once kiddish had attained maturity. I would have cried if he had made me field like this yesterday. The gulli toured two hundred yards when he clacked it with his danda.

One of the fielders tried to cheat. He thought he had caught the gulli. Gaya said that the gulli had first hit the ground. They were about to come to fight. But the young boy stepped out when he saw Gaya's face filled with anger. Had he not backed out, there would have been a fight. Although I was not playing, I was enjoying it all. It reminded me of the good old days of boyhood. Now I realized that yesterday Gaya only pretended to be playing. He had taken mercy on me. I had cheated but he didn't lose his temper, because he was not playing but only pretending. He didn't want to torture me by making me chase the gulli endlessly. I was an officer and this officership had become a wall between us. Now I could get his respect or his services but not his companionship. During our childhood days, we were equals. There was no distance between us. But now in this position, I was an object of his pity. He didn't accept me as his equal. He had grown taller and I had grown smaller.

4. The Story of Two Bullocks

1

The male ass is thought to be the most stupid of animals. Whenever we want to say that someone is a fool of the first order we call him an ass. One cannot really say whether the jackass is really stupid, or his harmless nature has crowned him with this title. Cows hit with their horns, and a married one can easily assume the title of a lioness. A dog is also a humble creature, but he too feels angry at times. One has, however, never heard of or seen a jackass getting into a fight. Whip him as much as you want, give him the worst kind of grass that has gone stale—but you will never see the slightest trace of discontent on his face. He might enjoy around a bit in the month of Baisakh, but I have never seen a jackass be truly happy. Satisfaction rests on his face permanently. He is not affected by moments of joy or sorrow, profit or loss. The attributes of angels and sages seem to have reached their climax in the jackass, yet people call him an idiot. Such disrespect for virtue cannot be seen anywhere else. Sometimes, simplicity is of no use in this world. See! Why are the Indians in Africa in such a pitiable state? Why aren't they permitted to enter America? The poor fellows do not consume liquor, they save up money for bad times, they work hard and never get into a fight with anyone. Even when insulted they do not fight back, yet they are dubbed with a bad name. It is said that they lower the standard of living. If they had learnt to retaliate they would have been called civilized. Take the example of Japan—a single success and they are now counted among the civilized nations of the world.

But jackass has a younger brother who is only a little less unwise in comparison, and that is bullock. We use the phrase 'calf's uncle' more or less to mean the same as a jackass. There are some people who might call a bullock the greatest of all fools, but our perspective is different. Sometimes bullock hits back, and one also witnesses an angry bullock. In many other ways he does express his discontent; hence, he is placed on a lower pedestal than a jackass.

Jhuri, the vegetable farmer, had named his two bullocks, Hira and Moti. They were mainly western—nice-looking, of good built and light-footed in work. Having lived together for a long time, the bullocks had been like brothers. Facing each other or sitting side by side, they would exchange their views through mute actions. How one got to know the other's feelings we cannot say. They must have been bestowed with a secret power, not known to humans who boast to be the noblest of all beings. They show their love by licking and sniffing each other. Sometimes they would cross their horns, not in enmity but in love and affection, just as intimate friends hug or pat each other's backs firmly. Without it, friendship lacks verve, as if it was superficial and cannot be trusted. When these two were put together in the harrow or the cart and they walked together swinging their necks, each trained to carry the greater part of the work on his shoulder. After the day's work, they would be untied in the afternoon or the evening and would relax by licking one another. When oilcake and straw were thrown into the trough they would stand up together, thrust their snouts into the crib and then sit side by side. When one took out his mouth from the trough, the other did the same.

It happened on one fine day that Jhuri sent the bullocks to his father-in-law's house. Now, how would the bullocks know why they have been parted away? They thought that their master had sold them. No one realised whether they liked being sent off in this way, but Jhuri's brother-in-law, Gaya, had a hard time managing them. If he shouted from behind they would run right or left, and if he pulled them holding the rope from the front they would go back. If he beat them they would lower their heads and snort. If God had given them the power to speak, they would have asked Jhuri, 'Why are you steering us, poor unfortunates, away? We have tried our best to serve you. If you were not contented with our work, we could've worked harder. We would have loved to die in your service. We never said anything about the fodder. We consumed whatever you gave us. Then why did you sell us off to this despot?'

The two came to their new home in the evening. They had been fasting the whole day but when they were brought to the manger, neither of them even sniffed the fodder. Their hearts were heavy; they had been separated from the place they regarded as home. Altogether a new house, a new village, and new people seemed alien to them.

They asked each other in mute language, looked at each other from the corners of their eyes and then lay down. When the whole village was in deep sleep, they pulled hard, broke the rope and set out for home. The rope was a strong one and no one could have realised that any bullock could cut it. But the two bullocks gathered their strength, pulled hard and the rope surrendered to their violent jerks.

When Jhuri got up in the morning he saw the two bullocks standing at the trough, a part of the rope was still dangling from their necks. Their legs were covered with muck up to their knees and their eyes shone with rebellious affection.

Seeing this, his heart was filled with warmth. He went straight to the trough and threw his arms around them. It was such a heartening sight to see them hugging and kissing each other.

The children of the house and the villagers gathered there and welcomed the bullocks by clapping their hands. This incident, though not an example in the village, had its value. The gathering of boys thought that these two animal-heroes must be celebrated. They brought bread, molasses, bran and chaff from their houses.

One of them said, 'No one has bullocks like these.'

Another boy replied, 'Yes indeed. They managed to come back from so far on their own.'

A third one came in, 'They aren't bullocks. They must have been human beings in their earlier birth.'

This statement remained undisputed.

When Jhuri's wife got to know about the bullocks at the door she flared up. 'How ungrateful these bullocks are! They didn't work even for a day before running away.'

Jhuri did not want to listen to these allegations thrown at his bullocks. 'Why are you calling them ungrateful? Your people must not have fed them, so what could they do?'

His wife said angrily, 'Yes, it is only you who know how to feed the bullocks. Other people only give water to their animals.'

Jhuri made fun of her, 'Why would they run off if they were given food?'

His wife was annoyed. 'They ran off because my people do not kindle them like fools as you do. If they feed them, they also make them work hard. These two are good for nothing, and that is why they ran away. Now, I'll look who gives them oilcake and bran. I'll give them only dry straws. They can eat it or die!'

This is exactly what happened. The servants were instructed that the bullocks should not be given anything but dry straw.

When the bullocks put their mouths in the trough their food seemed dry. No flavour, no juice. How could they eat this? They began to stare at the door with longing eyes.

Jhuri said to a servant, 'Hey, why aren't you giving them oilseeds?'

'The mistress will kill me.'

'You can do it trickily.'

'No, sir. Later, you'll also join her.'

2

Jhuri's brother-in-law arrived the next day and took away the bullocks. This time he yoked them both to his cart. Twice or thrice Moti tried to pull the cart to the ditch along the road but Hira held him back. Hira was more patient.

Reaching home in the evening, Gaya tied them with thick ropes as a punishment for the previous day's mischief. Then he threw the same dry straw at them. To his own two bullocks, he gave oilcake and other delicacies.

The bullocks had never faced such humiliation. Jhuri wouldn't strike them even with a flower-twig. He would merely click his tongue and they would run. Here they were thrashed. Their honour was bruised; on top of it, they were given only dry straw to eat.

They didn't even look at the trough.

The next day Gaya yoked them to the plough. But it was as if they had sworn not to budge from where they stood. Once when the cruel fellow struck Hira on his nostrils, Moti went mad with rage and ran away with the plough. The ploughshare, the yoke, the rope, and the harness were all smashed to pieces. But there were thick ropes around their necks and so no one could catch them.

Hira said silently, 'It is useless to run away.'

Moti replied, 'But he almost killed you.'

'Now he'll beat us to his heart's content.'

'Let him. We were born bullocks, how long can we escape beating?'

'Gaya is running towards us with two other fellows. They've sticks in their hands.'

Moti said, 'Shall I show him a few tricks? He's coming with a stick.'

Hira reasoned with him, 'No, brother. Stand still.'

'If he beats me, I'll knock one or two down.'

'No. This isn't our dharma[22].'

Moti stood there resentfully. Gaya arrived and led them away. Fortunately, he didn't beat them, for if he had, Moti would have struck back. Seeing his frown, Gaya and his companions decided that it was better to put it off this time.

---

22. Duty

The same dry straw was thrown at them again, but they stood still. The people in the house got to have their meal. At that moment, a small girl came out with two chapattis in her hand. She gave them the chapattis and went away. One chapatti was barely sufficient to satisfy their hunger but they felt a sense of contentment in their hearts. Here, too, there was someone decent and humane. She was Bhairo's daughter who had lost her mother. Her stepmother used to beat her often, which is why she was kind to the bullocks.

Both remained fastened to the plough throughout the day, were beaten and sometimes they acted stupidly. In the evening, they were tied up at the same place, and at night the same small girl fed them two chapattis. For them, it was an honourable meal, filled with love, which gave them strength so that they don't grow weak by eating their daily dose of a little straw. But their eyes and every part of their body sought revenge.

One day, Moti said silently, 'I can't take it anymore, Hira.'

'What do you want to do?'

'I want to lift one or two with my horns and throw them.'

'You know very well that the owner of this house is the father of the dear girl who feeds us chapattis. Won't the poor girl become an orphan?'

'Should I throw the stepmother, then? It is she who beats the girl.'

'You're forgetting that it is not in our rules to strike womankind.'

'You've kept no way out for me, answer me, shall we break the rope and run off?'

'Yes, I'd agree to that. But how can such a strong rope be broken?'

'There's a way. Chew the rope at first a little, and then pull.'

At night when the girl left after feeding them chapattis, both started chewing the rope. But the big rope was too strong for them. They tried again and again without any luck.

Suddenly the door opened and the girl came out. Both lowered their heads and began to lick the girl's palm. Their tails raised as she touched their foreheads. Then she said, 'I'm opening the rope. You must get away quietly, or these people will murder you. Today, they were talking about putting rings in your noses.'

She untied the knot, but they stood there unmoved.

Moti said silently, 'Why are you not moving?'

Hira said, 'We can get away, but tomorrow this girl will be in trouble. Everyone will suspect her.'

Suddenly the girl cried out, 'Uncle's bullocks are running away! Daddy, daddy, hurry up! They're running off!'

Gaya rushed out of the house and ran to get hold of the bullocks. They pushed Gaya out with force and ran quickly. Gaya raised an alarm. Then he went back to bring some people from the village. The two friends took the opportunity to make their escape. They ran straight ahead, unmindful of the right way. They could not find any clue of the path they had come through. They went through new villages. Then they stood at the side of a field and started to think about what should be done next.

Hira said, 'It seems we have lost our way.'

'You ran without having the right thought. We should have killed him right there.'

'If that was done what would the people say? He abandoned his dharma, why should we abandon ours?'

The two bullocks were very hungry. There were peas growing in the field beside them. They began to chomp them, and at times stopped to listen if anyone was coming.

When they had had their fill they were overwhelmed by their newly attained independence and began to prance and jump about. First, they gushed, and then they locked their horns and started pushing one another. Moti plunged Hira back several steps until he fell into a ditch. That made Hira annoyed. He somehow managed to get up and collided with Moti. He observed that what started as a game was getting into a fight and moved aside.

3

Now, what did they see? A raging bull was heading toward them. Yes, indeed, it was a bull and it had almost reached where they stood. The two friends were in a tight spot and looked for an escape route. The bull looked as if he was a real elephant. To clash with him would be fatal. But even if they did not clash with him, there did not seem to be any chance of their survival. He was heading straight towards them. It was a ghastly sight!

Moti said silently, 'We are in a mess. Can we save our skin? Think of some way!'

Hira said in a worried voice, 'He is blind with pride and won't listen to our pleas.'

'Let's run.'

'Running away is cowardice.'

'Then you be here to die. I'm taking to my heels.'

'And, if he chases us?'

'Then think of something else.'

'The only solution is if we pounce on him together at once. I'll lead the attack from the front, you take him from behind. If he is cornered from both sides, he'll flee. If he jumps on me, you thrust your horns in his belly from the side. Our lives are on the line, but there's no other way.'

Gathering all their courage the two friends mounted their attack. The bull had no experience of facing a united army. He was accustomed to fighting duels. The moment he leapt at Hira, Moti gave him a chase from behind. The bull turned back to face him when Hira pounced on him. The bull wanted to knock them down one by one, but these two were masters of their craft and did not give him the opportunity. Infuriated by this two-pronged attack, the bull at one point moved threateningly towards Hira, determined to attack him, but right at that moment Moti came from sideways and put his horns into his belly. The bull became furious and as he turned back Hira attacked him with his horns from the other side. Badly injured, the bull took to his heels and the two friends chased him for quite some distance until the bull collapsed on the ground, unconscious. Then they left him.

Intoxicated by their victory the two friends walked triumphantly, swinging from side to side.

Moti said in his symbolic language, 'I really wanted to finish off the fellow.'

Heera reprimanded him, 'One should not strike a fallen enemy.'

'This is rubbish. The enemy should be struck down in a way that he does not rise again.'

'Now, how to get back home—think about that.'

'Let's first eat something and think later.'

The pea field was spread right before them. Moti went right in. Hira forbade him but he didn't listen. He had barely taken two or three morsels when two men appeared with sticks and surrounded the two friends. Hira was standing on the embankment and ran away, but Moti was deep in the lush field. His hooves got stuck in the mud so he could not get out and was caught. When Hira saw that his friend was in trouble he came back. If they were going to be trapped, they would be trapped together. The watchmen caught him too.

In the morning, the two friends were shut in a pinfold.

4

The whole day passed away and they were not fed with even a single straw—this was the first time that such a thing was happening to them. They were not able to understand what kind of a master this was. There were many buffaloes, goats, horses and donkeys, but there was no fodder in front of anyone. All were lying on the ground like culprits as if they had committed some crime. Some of them were so lean that they could not even get up. The two friends kept their eyes fixed at the gate the entire day but no one came with food. Then both started to lick the sultry clay of the wall but that could not bring them any relief.

When they were not given any food in the evening too, Hira's heart burned with anger. He said to Moti, 'I can't bear it anymore.'

His head lowered, Moti answered, 'I feel as though my life is waning out.'

'Don't give up so quickly, buddy. We must find some way of getting out of here.'

'Come, let's break the wall.'

'I'm not good for anything now.'

'Well, why did you then boast about your strength?'

'All that is out of me now.'

The wall of the compound was built of clay. Hira was strong, he pointed his horn against the wall. When he dug deeper a big chunk of clay loosened. This encouraged him to push the wall again and again. Running again and again he hit the wall and with every blow, he knocked off little chunks of clay from the wall.

Right at that time, the watchman came with a lantern in his hand on his regular rounds to count the animals. When he saw Hira causing a ruckus, he beat him several blows and then held him up with a thick rope.

Moti said lying from his place, 'What did you get out of it but blows?'

'Well, at least I tried to use my power.'

'Was that of any use? Now you have been tied up.'

'Well, we must use our strength whatever the pros and cons.'

'That will cost you your life in the end.'

'I don't give a damn! We're going to die after all. Just think if the wall had fallen, it could have saved many lives. So many of our brothers are tied up here. There is barely any life left in their bodies. If it continues like this for a few more days, they'll all die.'

'That's correct. All right then, let me also use my power.'

Moti also banged against the wall at the same spot. A chunk of clay came down which gave him more strength. He began to bang the wall repeatedly as though it was his sparring partner. Finally, after about two hours of tussle, the top of the wall came down by about a foot and a half. He put the final blow with doubled strength and this time half of the wall came down swinging.

As soon as the wall fell, the animals that had been lying down like prisoners for so long got up. The three mares galloped away first, followed by the goats. Then the buffaloes slipped away, but the donkeys still lying there did not move.

Hira asked, 'Why aren't you two going away?'

One of them replied, 'What if we get caught up again?'

'What does it matter? At least now you've got the opportunity to run away.'

'We're frightened. We'd rather stay here.'

Midnight has just passed. The two donkeys were still thinking about whether they should escape or not. Moti was busy trying to chew his friend's rope. When he could not, Hira said, 'You leave. Let me be here. Maybe, we'll meet again sometime.'

With watery eyes, Moti said, 'Do you think I'm so self-centred, Hira? You and I have been with each other for such a long time! If you're in danger today can I just go away and leave you all alone?'

Hira said, 'They'll bash you really hard. They will know that it's your handiwork.'

Moti said proudly, 'If I get beaten for the crime that I have committed, I don't give a damn. At least the lives of nine or ten animals have been saved. They'll bless us.'

Saying this Moti hit the two donkeys with his horns and put them out of the compound. Then he lay beside his friend and went to sleep.

There is no need to discuss the terrible scene that followed in the morning when the clerk, the watchman and the other administrators saw what had happened. It is sufficient to say that Moti was roundly thrashed and he too was tied up with a thick rope.

5

For a whole week, the two friends stayed tied up there. They were not given a single morsel of straw to eat. Only once they were given water which barely kept them alive. They grew so lean that they could hardly stand, and their ribs budged out of their skin.

One day, the sound of drums was heard in front of the courtyard, and by noon about fifty to sixty people gathered there. The inspection began and the two companions were taken out. People came to have a look at them and went back dissatisfied. No one would be interested in buying bullocks that looked like dead bodies.

Suddenly a bearded man came there whose eyes were red and who had a rough look. He poked his fingers at the thighs of the bullocks and began to talk with the clerk. The appearance of the man terrified the two friends. They had no doubt who he was and why he was touching their bodies. They looked at each other with scared eyes and lowered their heads.

Hira said, 'It was useless to run away from Gaya's house. Our heads won't be saved now. Moti said disdainfully, 'everyone says, God is kind to everybody. Why isn't He generous to us?'

'For God, it does not matter whether we live or die. In a way, it's good that for a while we'll be with Him. Once God had saved us in the form of that little girl. Won't He save us now?'

'This man is going to cut us with his knife. Just watch out.'

'Well, why are we disheartened? Our flesh, hide, horns and bones, everything will be of use to someone or the other.'

After the auction, the bearded man took both friends with him. Every bone of their bodies shivered in fear. They had no power to lift their hooves but they were so scared that they swayed along—for if they slowed down a little, the fellow would give them a brutal bash.

Along the way, they saw a lush green meadow where cows and bullocks were grazing. All the animals were in a good mood, good-looking and happily fed. Some were leaping while others were happily chewing the cud sitting idly. How joyous they were! And how selfish! In their blessed state, they did not care that two of their brothers . . .

Suddenly it seemed to them that the road was known. Yes, it was the same road by which Gaya had taken them away. It was the same fields, orchards and villages. With every step, they hastened. Their tiredness and weakness fled away. Oh, look, here was their own land, and this was the well from which they drew water by pulling the crane. It was the same well!

Moti said, 'Our house is nearby.'

'It's all God's generosity,' responded Hira.

'I'm running for home.'

'Will he permit you?'

'I'll thump him down.'

'Oh no! Let's run and reach our stalls, and we won't move from there.'

They seemed to go crazy with delight, and like calves, leapt and ran towards the house. 'That's our stand!' They reached the spot and stood there. The bearded fellow also followed them.

Jhuri was seated in his doorway taking a sun bath. As soon as he looked at the bullocks he rushed to them and began hugging them over and over again. Tears of happiness rolled down the eyes of the two friends, and one of them started licking Jhuri's hand.

The bearded fellow followed up and snatched the rope tied to the bullocks' necks.

Jhuri came up, 'They are my bullocks.'

'They cannot be yours? I bought them over in the auction at the animal farm.'

'I think you have stolen them,' said Jhuri. 'Just leave silently. They are my bullocks. Only I have the right to sell them. No one else has the right to put my bullocks on sale in an auction.'

'I'll complain at the police station.'

'They're mine. It's proof that they're standing at my door.'

Infuriated, the bearded fellow came forward and tried to drag the bullocks by force. Right at that moment, Moti struck him with his horns. The fellow stepped back. Moti chased him. He stopped only when he drove the fellow out of the village, and then stood there guarding the way. The man stood at some distance threatening, cursing and pelting stones at Moti. And Moti stood there like a victorious hero, blocking the way. The villagers had gathered there to see the spectacle and had a hearty laugh.

It was only when the man admitted defeat and went away Moti walked back swaggering.

Hira said, 'I was afraid you might hit him off in anger.'

'If he had grabbed me, I would've certainly killed him.'

'He won't be back now.'

'If he does, I'll take care of him. I'll see how he takes us away.'

'What if he gets us shot?'

'Well, I'll die but I'll be of no use to him.'

'Nobody thinks our life is worth anything.'

'Just because we're so simple.'

Soon their trough was filled with oilseed cakes, straw, bran and grain, and the two friends began to eat. Jhuri looked at them affectionately and the gang of boys around witnessed this tender sight.

Just then the mistress of the house came out and kissed the two on their foreheads.

5. An Innocent Friend

A bird had laid eggs just above the cornice in Keshav's house. Both Keshav and his sister, Shyama, would watch the bird intently, as it flew back and forth. The first thing every morning the two would come and stand in front of the cornice, rubbing their eyes, barely awake. The pleasure they drew from seeing the two birds living there was so great that they even forgot about the joys of milk and jalebi[23]. Countless questions came into their minds: How big were the eggs? What colour were they? How many? What did they eat? How would the chicks come out of them? What is the nest like? But they both found no one to answer their queries. Their mother had no time to spare from the housework and their father from his books. The two children had to comfort themselves by asking and answering each other.

Shyama: 'Tell me, bhaiya, will the chicks fly away as soon as they are hatched?'

'No, silly,' Keshav would reply, proud as a professor. 'First, their wings will grow. How would the small beings fly without wings?'

Shyama: 'What would the little one be given to eat by their poor mother?' This was a difficult question for even Keshav to answer.

---

23. A sweet

A couple of days went by and the children's excitement went up. They were eager to look at the eggs. They were sure the chicks had come out by then. The question of what the chicks would feed on now lay heavily on their minds.

From where would the poor bird find enough grain to feed her little ones? The chicks were sure to starve to death.

This thought left the siblings very curious. They decided to scatter some grain on the cornice for the birds to pick up. Shyama said happily, 'Oh! Then the bird won't have to fly anywhere in search of food, will she?'

'Oh no!' said Keshav 'Why would she?'

'But won't the chicks be really warm up there?' a new question crossed Shyama's mind.

Keshav had no idea of this situation until then. 'Yes!' he said. 'Might be they are dying of thirst up there. There is no shade above them even.'

It was finally decided that an artificial roof would be put above the nest. A bowl of water and some grains of rice were also to be kept up there.

Both children began to work honestly. Shyama silently brought some rice from the clay pot. Keshav quietly emptied the stone bowl of its oil, and after scrubbing and cleaning refilled it with water.

But where could they get the cloth for the shelter? And how to make the roof stay up there without support? Keshav was slightly puzzled over the problem for a while before it was finally resolved. 'Go and bring the garbage basket, make sure Ma is not able to see you.'

'But it has a hole in the middle! Will it keep the sunlight away?'

'First, bring the basket,' Keshav said with a little annoyance. 'I'll take care of the hole.'

Shyama went hastily and came back with the basket. Keshav filled the hole with some paper and seated the basket in front of the branch of a close tree nearby. 'See, how the shadow of the basket falls on the nest! The sun can't peep in now!'

Shyama admired the cleverness of his brother.

***

It was the summer months. Their father was out to work. Having put both children to sleep, the mother had lied down to rest. But the kids were not interested in sleeping. Eyes closed, they held their breath and waited for the right moment. As soon as they made sure their mother was asleep, they got up silently, unlocked the door, and went out. Soon they were making arrangements to safeguard the eggs. Keshav took a stool from the room, but it was still not high enough to reach the cornice. He then brought a small bathroom stool to keep it under the first and carefully reached the top.

With both hands, Shyama held the stool. Its legs were uneven which made it rather unstable, and it inclined to whichever side the pressure increased. Only Keshav knew what anxiety, what fear troubled him at that moment. He would hold the cornice to balance himself, and remarked Shyama under his breath, 'Hold tight or I'll come down and bang you niccly.' But poor Shyama's heed was taken up by the cornice. Time and again her mind weaved in that direction, and her grasp on the stool released.

The moment Keshav's hands got to the cornice, the birds flew away. Keshav saw some twigs scattered on the cornice, and three eggs lying on them. The nest was not like the ones he had seen on trees. Shyama asked, 'Can you spot any chicks, bhaiya?'

'There are three eggs; the chicks haven't hatched yet.'

'Show me, bhaiya! How big are they?'

'I will. But first bring some rags to lay under the eggs. The poor eggs are being placed on twigs and straw.'

Shyama ran out and came back with a piece of cloth torn out from an old sari. Keshav bent to take it from her, folded it a number of times to make it cushion-like and put it under the eggs.

'I also want to look at them, bhaiya,' Shyama requested.

'Yes, yes. I will show them to you. But first bring the basket so that a roof can be made,' answered Keshav.

Shyama passed the basket from beneath and said, it's my turn now, you come down.

Keshav seated the basket against the branch and said, 'Go and bring the water and grain. Let me get down and then you can have a look.'

Shyama brought the bowl of water and rice too. Keshav placed them both under the basket and came down softly. Shyama begged once again, 'Bhaiya, help me climb up too so I can see!'

'You'll fall down.'

'I won't fall down, bhaiya! You hold the stool.'

'No, No, No, if you fall down, Ma will beat me to a pulp. She will accuse me of helping you. What will come out of your seeing them, anyway? Now the eggs are comfortable. When they hatch, we'll both look after the chicks.'

The two birds approached the cornice only to quickly fly away again.

Keshav wondered if they were scared and he took away the stools. Shyama was tearful.

'You didn't show me!' she complained, 'I'll tell Ma.'

'I'll bash you if you tell Ma.'

'Then why didn't you show me?'

'And what if you had fallen down and smashed your head?'

'So what! Big deal! You just wait, I'll tell Ma.'

Just then the door opened and the mother came out, shielding her eyes from the blazing sun. 'What are you two doing out there in the sun?' she asked. 'Who opened the latch? How many times do I have to tell you not to come out in the afternoon?'

Keshav had unfastened the latch, but Shyama did not carp that to mother. She was frightened that he might get a beating. Keshav was scared that Shyama might scream. He had not shown her the eggs and therefore did not trust her. Whether Shyama did not speak out of love or because she was party to the fault is a matter of speculation. Perhaps it was both.

The mother rebuked, took hold of both of them and took them back inside the room. She locked the door and started fanning them quietly. It was only two o'clock in the afternoon and the hot summer wind was blowing outside. Soon, the two kids were sleeping soundly.

Shyama woke up at four o'clock. The door was unlocked. She ran to the eave and looked up. There was no indication of the basket. She looked down for a possibility, hurried back to the room and shouted, 'Bhaiya, the eggs have fallen down, the chicks have flown away.'

Keshav ran to the cornice and saw that the three eggs were lying damaged on the floor. A slimy white and yellow liquid was coming out of them. The bowl of water was also lying upturned.

Keshav went pale and stared at the ground with soggy eyes.

'Where have the chicks flown to?' Shyama asked.

'The eggs are broken,' Keshav said sadly.

'And where have the chicks gone?'

'Where do you think!' he replied with some irritation. 'Can't you see the white liquid coming out? It would have turned into chicks in a few days.'

The mother shouted from behind, 'what are you two doing out in the sun?'

'Ma! Ma! The eggs are broken,' said Shyama.

'You must have fiddled with them,' said the mother angrily, looking at the broken shells.

Now Shyama had no pity for her brother. He must not have put the eggs back delicately enough and so they had rolled off. He needed to be punished.

Shyama said, 'Ma, he touched the eggs.'

'Why?' the mother enquired.

Keshav stood tongue-tied.

'How did you go up there?' the mother asked again.

'He kept a stool on the bathing stool and climbed up,' Shyama said.

'Weren't you holding the stool?' Keshav charged.

'You asked me to!' replied Shyama.

'You are a big boy, Keshav,' said the mother. 'Don't you know that when you touch birds' eggs they become infected, and then the birds don't look after them anymore?'

'So the birds have put down the eggs themselves!' Shyama asked her mother fearfully.

'What else would the birds do?' the mother said. 'Keshav, you have done a horrific thing. Oh my God! Three lives have been taken by you!'

Keshav looked sad. 'I only protected the eggs,' he said silently.

The mother laughed at this. For quite some time after this incident, Keshav was nailed by a guilty conscience. In trying to protect the eggs, he had damaged them, this thought would even make him cry sometimes.

But the two birds were never seen there again.

6. Big Brother

My brother was five years older than me, but only three classes ahead. He started studying at the same age as I did but he didn't want to hurry with matters of great importance such as education. He wanted to build on a strong foundation. So he took two years to do what could be done in one year. If the groundwork was not well done, how could a building be sturdy?

I was younger. I was nine; he was fourteen. To look over me and keep an eye on me was his birthright. And my integrity was in following his instructions as if it was the Law.

He was studious by nature. He always sat with an open book in front of him. Sometimes, to rest his brain, he would draw pictures of birds, dogs or cats in the margins of his books and notebooks. Sometimes, he would write the same name or word or sentence over and over again. Sometimes, he would write a line of poetry in beautiful handwriting. Sometimes, he would write things that had neither meaning nor sense. Once, I saw the following written in his copy: Special, Ameena, Brothers-Brothers, Actually, Brother-Brother, Radhe-Shyam, Mr Radheshyam, For One Hour. And after this, he had made a drawing of a man. I tried my best to make sense of this riddle but I couldn't. I didn't have the confidence to ask him. After all, he was in the ninth standard; I was only in the fifth. How could I have understood what he had written?

I was not at all interested in studying. Sitting with a book for even one hour made me uneasy. And the first chance I got, I would flee from the hostel and go to the playground to play with marbles, sometimes fly paper butterflies, and my day would be made if a friend appeared. We would climb up on the roof and take turns jumping off, or swing on the gate and claim it was a motor car. But the moment I would enter the room and see Big Brother, or Big B's angry face, I would get scared to death. His first question used to be: 'Where were you?' The question was always asked in the same tone and my answer was always silence. I don't know why I could never answer that I was out, playing. My silence indicated that I accept my crime and Big B would have no other option but to greet me with words that showed both his love and anger:

'If you continue to study English like this, you can go on trying for the rest of your life and you still won't learn a word. Studying the English language is not a joke; everyone can't master it. Or else every Tom, Dick and Harry would be a genius of English. You have to toil day and night to learn it, and you can never fully grasp it either. All sorts of learned men can't actually write, let alone speak in English. And you are such an idiot that you don't learn from my example. You can see for yourself how hard I work. And if you can't see, you are blind and stupid. Every day there is a play or a festival. Have you ever seen me go to even one of them? Every day there is a hockey or a cricket match. I never go anywhere near them. I am always studying, yet I end up studying in the same class for two, sometimes even three years. Then, how do you expect to pass despite wasting all your time on fun and games? Do you want to spend the rest of your life in the same class? If this is the way you want to waste your life, you may go back home and play gulli-danda. Why are you wasting our poor father's hard-earned money?'

I would listen to this deride and start crying. I had no answer. I was guilty and charged. Big B was expert at lambasting. He could say such hard-hitting things, aim such prickly arrows that my heart would break into pieces and my confidence would shatter. Yet I didn't have the physical strength for such do-or-die labour. At such times of distress, I would think, 'Maybe it is best to go back home. Why should I take on something that is beyond my abilities and destroy my life? I am willing to stay illiterate.' The very thought of so much hard work would make my head spin. In an hour or two, the clouds of desperation would flee and I would decide to study hard. I would make a time-table. After all, how could I begin to work without first drawing up a map or a plan? There was no space for games and sports in this time-table. According to this plan, I would wake up at 6 A.M., wash, have my breakfast and sit down to study. From six to eight, time to study English; eight to nine Maths; nine to nine-thirty History; then have my mid-day meal and go to school. I would get back from school at half-past three, leisure for half an hour, then study Geography from four to five, Grammar from five to six, walk for half an hour in front of the hostel; study English composition from six-thirty to seven; translation from eight to nine after dinner; Hindi from nine to ten; different subjects from ten to eleven; and then go to sleep.

But to make a time-table and to follow it are two different things. Rules would be broken from the very first day. The temptation of a green sports field, the sweet breeze that blew there, the joy of running after the football, the pick-and-throw of kabaddi, and the speed and sureness of volleyball would pull me in strange and unknown ways. Once on the sports field, I would forget everything else. That murderous time-table, those books that would blind me one day—I would remember nothing. And Big B would get yet another occasion to give his lecture. I began to run from the very sight of him. I would try my best to stay away from his omnipresent eyes. Howsoever silently I entered the room he spotted me. The moment he looked in my direction, I could feel my life waning out of me. I constantly felt as though a sword is trailing above my head. But just as humans remain caught up in the affairs of the world even at a time of trouble or death, my interest in fun and games remained unabated despite the scoldings and insults.

2

Soon the yearly exams began. Big B could not pass; I could not only get through but also stood first in my class. Now there was only a difference of two classes between him and me. There were many things I wanted to tell Big B: 'What about all your hard work? Look at me; I was having all the fun playing and then also stood first in my class.'

But he was so downcast that I truly repented for him and the thought of rubbing salt on his wounds seemed an awful thing to me. However, I grew in confidence and pride. And with it, Big B's awe diminished. I started taking part in fun and games with a greater sense of liberation. I had decided: if he ever tries to give me a speech I shall tell him what I think. I shall say, 'What have you achieved after all the long hours of hard work? Look at me, I loitered all day and yet I came first in my class!' Though I didn't have the strength to actually say these words aloud, it was evident from my behaviour that Big B's days of despotic rule over me were a thing of the past.

Big B sensed it. He was quite clever in these simple matters. One day, when after playing gulli-danda all morning,

I returned for my meal, Big B was ready to attack. He pounced on me, 'I can see that passing this year and being first in your class has gone to your head. But, my dear brother, remember that many great men have lost their pride; you are nothing in comparison to them. You must have read about Ravana's fate. What have you learnt from reading about him? Or did you just read without understanding? Simply passing in History is not enough; the real thing is the growth and development of your brain. You must understand whatever you read. Ravana ruled over a large empire. Such kings are called Chakravartin kings, or supreme rulers. The English too ruled over large parts of the world but they cannot be called Chakravartin. Many countries do not accept the supremacy of the English; they remain independent and free. But Ravana was a chakravartin ruler. All other rulers paid him a tax. Even the gods obeyed him. Even the gods of fire and water accepted him as their master. Yet, what was Ravana's end? Pride caused him to fall. In the end, there was no one with him. A man may achieve any heights but he must not be proud. The day you become proud, your days are numbered.

'You must have read about Satan. He began to trust that there could be no big believer in God than him. In the end, he was driven out of Heaven and thrown into Hell. The Emperor of Rome too suffered from pride. He died as a beggar. You have only passed one class and it has entered your head. Don't forget, you have not passed because of hard work; it is only good luck, a matter of chance. But it won't happen every time. In gulli-danda sometimes you get a blind shot; you do not become an expert player by that. The expert player is one whose shots never go empty. Don't go by the fact that I have not passed. When you come to my standard you will know how difficult it is. When you have to study Algebra and Geometry, the History of England, and recall the names of the kings, all eight Henrys! Do you believe it is easy to remember which incident took place during which King Henry's rule? If you write Henry VIII instead of Henry VII you lose all your marks. You get nothing, not even a zero! Do you know anything? There were dozens of James, another dozen Williams and thousands of Charles. It is sufficient to make your head rotate. They couldn't even think of new names; instead, they kept substituting II, IV, V after the same name. I could have told them a million names, had someone asked me.

'And Geometry... Only god can save you from it! If instead of a b c, you write a c b you end up losing all your marks. No one ever asks these cruel examiners what is the difference between a b c and a c b? Why do they kill innocent students over pointless, silly things? Whether you eat rice, dal and roti or dal, rice and roti—what difference does it make? But do these examiners care? They want students to memorize every word that is written in the textbooks. And this learning by rote they have called Education. But what is the use of memorizing these pointless things? If you drop that perpendicular over this line, then the base will be double of the first line. Ask them what is the advantage or purpose. Whether it is double or half—how does it benefit me? But if you want to pass the exams you have to remember all these nonsensical details.

'Another time they say—write an essay on 'Punctuality' in two-three pages. You open your copy, pen in hand, and get lost in thought. Everyone knows that it is good to be punctual, it brings order and discipline to a person's life, punctuality is liked by all, and it is good for business. But how can you write four pages on this? What is the point of taking four pages to write something that can be said in one line? I call this stupidity. This is wasting time, not saving it. I think one should be given a chance to write as short as possible But, no, you have to cover four pages with ink, no matter how you do it. What is this if it isn't cruelty towards students? And to top it all, they say, 'Write in brief'! Write on 'Punctuality' but take four pages! Wonderful! It is like telling someone to run fast and slowly! Does it make any sense? Even a child knows it is silly but not these teachers. They think they are smart. But actually, they are stupid. You will know how tough it is when you come to my class. You are in the sky these days because you have stood first in your class. But you must listen to me. I may have failed but I am older than you. I have more experience of the world than you have. Listen carefully to what I have to say, or else you will repent.'

Luckily, it was time to be in school or nobody knows when that speech would have come to an end. My meal became tasteless. If I am dishonoured like this after passing, I wondered, what would be my fortune if I fail? I was frightened of the terrifying picture Big B had sketched— a huge amount of work had to be done in his class. It is a surprise that I didn't fly away from school after that lecture. But despite all the insults that had been piled upon me, my disinterest in books remained as usual. I lost any opportunity to play my games. I would study, but very little—just enough to finish the work assigned to me and save me from the teachers' scolding. The boost I had gained soon vanished and I went back to living like a guilty thief.

3

Once again the yearly examinations came around and it so came about that I passed once again and Big B failed yet again. I hadn't worked very laboriously but I don't know how I stood first in my class. I myself was surprised. Big B had done his level best. He had learned every word of the syllabus. He would read till ten in the night and then again from four in the morning and from six till nine before going to school. And yet he failed. I felt sorry for him. When the results were announced, he burst into tears. My own joy was minimised. If I had failed too, Big B would have been less unhappy but no one can overcome fate.

Now there was only one class difference between Big B and me. An unkind thought arose in my mind: If Big B were to fail yet again, he and I would be in the same class. How would he, then, scold me? But with a great deal of effort, I removed the wicked thought. After all, Big B scolded me for my own benefit. Although I hated his lectures when he was delivering them, yet I knew it was because of his constant preaching that I cleared one class after another, and that too with such good marks.

By now Big B had eased a lot. Several times, despite finding ample opportunities to scold me, he would hold on to his patience. Perhaps he had realized that he no longer had the right to scold me, or if he had the right then it was much minimized. My determination increased. I began to take an unfair edge of his tolerance. I started to trust that I would pass—whether I read or not—because luck was with me. And so, the little studying I used to do because of Big B's fright stopped. My latest hobby was kite-flying and my entire day would go by just doing that. But I still regarded Big B. So I would fly kites when he wasn't observing. The various problems relating to kite-flying—how to fix knots proficiently, how to cut the strings of competitors' kites, how to enter kite-flying competitions—were dealt with quietly. I didn't want Big B to think that my regard for him had diminished in any way.

One day, late in the evening, I was far away from the hostel, running wildly after a cut kite. My eyes were fixed on the sky and my heart was set on this traveller from the skies that was quietly marching towards the ground as though a divine spirit was indifferently about to get into a new body. An army of boys, equipped with long poles and thorny twigs, was heading to get hold of it. No one cared about anything else rather than the sweeping kite. It was just like as if all of us were flying with the kite through the skies and there were no cars, no trams, no lorries.

Suddenly, I collided with Big B who was perhaps getting back from the market. He caught hold of my hand then and there and spoke furiously, 'Aren't you ashamed of yourself—wandering here and there with these rascals after a valueless kite? Have you no sense? Don't you realise you are no longer in a lower standard? You are now in the Eighth class, just one standard behind me. You must give some value to your stand in life. There was a time when people cleared the Eighth standard and became Deputy Tehsildars. I know so many Middle School pass-outs who have been promoted to become top-class Deputy Magistrates and Superintendents. So many of our country's leaders and newspaper editors have cleared only the Eighth standard. Some of the most learned men supervised them whereas you—you who are studying in the same Eighth standard— go catching around after kites with a bunch of street rascals! I am disheartened by your thoughtlessness.

'You are intelligent, there is no doubt about it, but what good is that intelligence if it destroys our honour in ourselves? You must be thinking—I am only one class short of my elder brother and so he doesn't have the authority to say anything to me anymore. But you are not right. I am five years older than you. Even if you and I are studying in the same standard—and if I continue to get the same result I shall, no doubt, remain in the same class as you and maybe next year you will leave me to go into the next grade—the five-year difference between us shall always be there. Not you, not even almighty, can erase that difference.

'I am five years older than you and shall always be so. You can never match the experience I have of life and of this world—not even if you get through MA or a DPhil. and a DLitt. Books alone do not preach to us the sense of right or wrong; you get it from observing and understanding the world. Our mother at no time studied in any class and our father never studied beyond the Fifth or Sixth standard. You and I can get through everything there is to study in the entire world, but our parents will always have the right to rebuke and correct us. Not because they have brought us to this world, but because they have far more experience of the world and shall always remain more experienced than us. What kind of government is there in America? Or how many times did Henry VIII marry, or the number of planets there are in the universe—they may not know these things, but there are thousands of other things they know that you and I do not.

'God forbid, if I were to fall ill today, wouldn't you fear? You would be able to do nothing except write a telegram to our father. But if our father were here in place of you, he wouldn't send any telegram anywhere; he would neither worry nor be nervous. He will first try to understand the cause and cure it as best as he can; if he doesn't succeed he will send for a doctor. Forget getting ill, you and I don't even know how to plan a month's expenses to last an entire month. Whatever our father sends us each month gets finished by the 20th or the 22nd and we are left with nothing.

Our breakfast stops. We have to avoid the washerman and the barber whereas our father has been spending less than half of what we spend in a month for his entire life. Not only has he lived well and with pride but he has managed a large family which includes nine dependents. 'Have a look at our Headmaster . . . He has done an MA and that too from Oxford. He obtains a thousand rupees, but who manages his home? His elderly mother! His degree is of no value in this field. He used to manage his household on his own earlier but the money would always be short. He was always on dues. Ever since his mother has taken over the charge, it is as though Goddess Lakshmi has been to their home. So, my dear brother, you must get rid of this ego that you have come closer to my grade and are, therefore, free to do as you want. I can'—(raises his hand as if to slap) — 'use this too. You do not like my words right now, don't you?'

In light of this new justification, I lowered my head with shame. In front of Big B, I felt really small. Real respect for him bulged in my heart. I spoke with water in my eyes, 'No, not at all. Each word you say is true and you have all the right to say it.'

Big B hugged me to his heart and said, 'I don't stop you from flying kites. I too sometimes feel like doing so, but what can I do? If I go far, how can I safeguard you? After all, that duty too rests on my head.'

By chance, at that very moment, a kite swayed over our heads. Its cut string trailed behind. A group of boys was running to catch it. Big B was tall; he jumped and caught hold of the string and began to run wildly towards the hostel. I ran after him.

7. A Night in the Month of Poos[24]

1

Halku came up to his wife and said, 'Sahna is here. Go, bring the money we've saved up. I'll give it to him and get rid of him.'

Munni was cleaning the floor. Turning around she said, 'There are just three rupees in all. If you hand it over, how will you get a blanket? Then how will you spend the chilly winter nights amidst the field? Tell him we'll settle after the harvest, not now.'

Halku stood there, undecided for a moment. The month of Poos, a chilly month, was soon to hit, and he could not remain in the field without a blanket. But Sahna wouldn't hear —he'd cast abuse and threats. If I passed away from the cold, let it be. At least, I'll clear out of this irritable person. Having this in mind, he moved his heavy body (ironic to his name) closer to his wife and said wheedling, 'Come on, get me the money and let me free my neck. I'll buy the blanket by finding some other means.'

Munni drew away from him, rolled her eyes and said, 'fed up with your means! Well, let me know about them. Will someone donate you a blanket out of charity? I don't know the amount

---

24. Poos or Paush is the 10th lunar month in Hindu calendar corresponding to the chilly winter months of December/January in the Gregorian calendar.

of the debt and why it simply can't be finished. I say, why don't you stop ploughing land? You overstrain yourself to death, if there is a good crop all of it goes to repay the debt and that's all. As if we're here only to repay debt. It's better to do day labour for our livelihood. Let thunder and lightning destroy such a harvest! I shan't give you the money — Never!'

Halku felt sad and said, 'Then shall I listen to him abuse me?'

Munni, knocked by his words, said, 'Why should he abuse you? We aren't his pupils!'

However, as soon as she said this, her worried eyebrows reduced.

The bitter truth hidden in Halku's words was glaring her in the face like a wild animal.

She went and brought the money from the shelf and handed it over to Halku. Then she said, 'You just stop digging the land from now on. As a labourer, at least you'll have your meal in peace. There won't be threats. We earn money through hard work, and throw it into the furnace and on top of it end up with such threats!'

Halku took the money and went out so reluctantly that it seemed as though he was taking out his heart and giving it over. He had managed to save three rupees from his wages with great difficulty. And he was going to part with that. His head lowered with a sense of impotence and infirmity.

2

The night of Poos was pitch black. Even the stars up there seemed to shiver. Halku sat under a shade of sugarcane leaves by his corn field and shivered in his old cotton wrap. Beneath the cot, his pet dog, Jabra, his only mate now, put his face in his belly and howled from the cold. None of them could sleep.

Pulling his knees closer to his chest Halku said to the dog, 'Hey, Jabra, are you feeling cold? I asked you to lie down on the straw at home but you came with me. Now face the cold, what can I do? You thought I'll munch on delicacies here, so you came running after me. Now face the music!'

Jabra lay there swinging his tail. Then he released a long whine, yawned and became quiet. He probably thought that his howling was not letting his master go to sleep.

Halku laid out his hand, ran it over Jabra's cold shoulders and said, 'Tomorrow no need to come with me, or you'll catch cold. This chilly west wind has become icy cold. I am going to fill the chillam[25]. Somehow I've to pass the night. I've had eight chillums already. This is the pleasure of working in the field! And there are those to whom the winter means nothing. Thick mattresses, quilts, blankets—they have every means to bear the cold. The cold doesn't dare come near them. The irony is that we do all the work and others have all the fun.'

Halku got up, picked up ash from the fire and filled his chillum. Jabra also sat up.

Halku smoked and said, 'You want to try? It can't scare away the cold; it's just a means to divert the mind.'

Jabra glared at him with longing eyes splashing with love.

Halku said, 'Bear the cold just for today. Tomorrow, I'll put some straw here. You can settle into it and won't feel the cold.'

On Halku's knees, Jabra put his front paws and got his face closer to his mouth. The warm breath of Jabra could be felt by Halku now.

Having smoked the chillum, Halku lay down again with the intention to sleep. But then his heartbeat increased. He

---

25. Pipe for smoking cannabis.

twisted and turned over. The terrible cold rest on his chest like the devil.

When he could not bear it any longer, he woke Jabra tenderly, tapped his head and made him lie down in his lap. The dog had a very bad smell but he clasped him close and experienced a solace he had not felt for the past several months. Jabra might have thought he was in heaven. And Halku's pure soul did not feel even a trace of hate for the dog. He held him as would have his most close friend or brother. He was not sad about the helplessness that had put him in this state. No! This unmatched friendship seemed to open all the doors of his soul, and each particle of his being overwhelmed with light.

Suddenly Jabra smelled the presence of an animal. This fired him with new energy and the cold wind became insignificant. He got up with full energy, left the shed and barked. Halku called after him many times with love. But he did not come back. He circled around the field and barked. If he did return any time, he would run back to his position the very next moment. His sense of duty did not permit him to sit for a moment.

3

As another hour passed, the night appeared to stir the cold wind. Halku got up and hid his head in his knees which were tugged up close to his heart. Yet, there was no relief from the cold. It looked as though his blood had iced, that instead of blood it was the ice that flowed in his veins. He glanced at the sky to gauge how much of the night was remaining. Saptarishi[26] had not yet covered half of its course in the sky. Only when it came overhead would dawn begin to break. The night was still young.

---

26. A constellation

Slightly further from Halku's field was a mango orchard. Autumn had rested in and the ground was sprinkled with fallen leaves. Halku thought of going there, collecting the leaves, lighting them, and getting himself heated by the fire. 'If anyone saw me collecting the leaves at night they would assume that I was a ghost. There could also be some wild animals hiding there. But I can't stay here in such a state any longer.'

He went up to the lentil field close by and took out a couple of plants. He made a broom out of them and holding a burning cow-dung cake in one hand, marched towards the orchard. Jabra started wagging his tail as he saw Halku coming closer to him.

Halku said, 'I can't bear it any more, Jabru. Come, let's collect some leaves from the orchard and warm ourselves. When we feel cosy, we'll come back and sleep. The night is yet to pass.'

Jabra howled in agreement and began to walk in front of Halku towards the orchard. It was pitch-dark around and the unkind wind swept over the leaves. Dewdrops were prickling down the trees making a tip-tap sound.

Suddenly a draught of wind flowed in with the scent of henna flowers.

Halku said, 'What a nice fragrance, Jabru! Do you also smell it?'

Jabra had found a bone and was busy biting it.

Halku put the lighted cow-dung cake down on the ground and started collecting the leaves. Soon, there was a huge heap. His hands were shivering; his bare feet seemed to be melting away. And he had made a huge pile. He would light the bonfire and bring it down to ashes.

Some seconds later the pile was lit up. The flames were so high that they were almost touching the leaves on the tree. In the restless light, the giant trees around looked as if carrying the darkness around on their head. In the unending sea of darkness, the flames appeared like a boat cruising softly through it.

Halku was warming himself resting by the fire. After some time, he took his sheet and put it beneath his arms. Then he stretched his legs as though he was posing a challenge to the wind to do its best. Having beaten the limitless power of the cold, he was finding it difficult to control his pleasure of victory. He said to Jabra, 'Hey Jabra, I hope you're not feeling cold anymore?'

Jabra whined as if to say, 'Do you think we are meant to feel perpetual cold or what?'

'Why didn't we think of it before? It would've saved us from the frosty cold.'

Jabra swaged his tail.

'Now, come and jump across the fire. Let's see who can do that. If you burn yourself, son, I am not going to apply balm to your wound.'

Jabra stared at the bonfire with longing eyes.

'Don't say anything to Munni tomorrow; she'll blow up a storm.'

Saying this, he crossed over the fire and landed safely on the other side. The flames scarcely licked his feet but that didn't matter. Jabra went around the fire and stood by his side.

Halku said, 'Come on, not in this manner. Jump over the fire.'

He jumped over it and got to the other side.

4

The leaves had been burnt to ashes. The orchard was again covered in darkness. The fire beneath the ashes would light up with each blow of wind. And then in the next second, it would be dark again.

Halku once again covered himself with the sheet and sitting beside the hot ashes, hummed a song. His body was warm now, but as the iciness intensified, he felt more and more inactive.

Suddenly, Jabra started to bark loudly and ran in the direction of the field. Halku doubted that a crowd of animals had drifted into his field. Probably, it was a bunch of antelopes. One could clearly hear them running all over the place. Then it seemed as if they were eating up the crop. He could hear them gnawing the cud.

He said to himself, 'No animal can get into the field while Jabra is around. He will shred them to pieces. I must be dreaming. See, nothing can be heard now. How I got misled!'

He called out loudly, 'Jabra, Jabra.'

Jabra continued to bark. He didn't come back to him.

Once again Halku heard the animals eating up the plants. He could no longer fool himself. He hated having to move from his place. How cosily he was sitting there! To go to the fields and run after the animals in the bitter cold was unbearable. He didn't move from his spot.

He called out louder, 'Jabra, Jabra.'

Jabra barked once again. The hungry animals were destroying the field. The harvest was ready to be cut. What a good crop it was! But these hungry animals were destroying it.

Halku made up his mind and took some steps. But soon a cold blow of wind bashed him like a scorpion's sting, and so he went back to the half-stamped-out fire. He pricked the ashes and stretched his limbs to warm them in the fire.

Jabra was now barking very loudly. The antelopes had cleared up the field and Halku was resting calmly beside the hot ashes. Inaction tied him like so many ropes from all around.

He fastened the sheet around him and lay down on the hot earth beside the ashes.

By the time he rose in the morning, the sun was up in the sky and had lit up the surroundings. Munni was saying, 'Will you keep on sleeping today? You are lying comfortably here and over there the entire crop has been destroyed.'

Halku got up and said, 'Have you come from the field?'

Munni said, 'Yes, the total field has been destroyed. And you're sleeping like a wood! What made you leave the shed?'

Halku made excuses. 'I was dying here, and you're only thinking about the field. I had such a bad stomach ache that I could think of nothing else.'

Both went to the field together and saw the entire field razed. And Jabra was lying down on earth under the shed. It seemed as though life had receded out of him.

Pain covered Munni's face. But Halku was happy.

Munni said thoughtfully, 'We'll have to work as wage earners to repay the debt now.'

Halku said light-heartedly, 'At least, now I'll not have to lie down here in the frozen nights.'

8. God resides in the Jury

1

Jumman Sheikh and Alagu Chaudhary were best friends. They worked their farms in partnership. They also had a business collaboration. Both had unbreakable faith in each other. When Jumaan went for Hajj, he had given the responsibility of looking after his household to Alagu; whenever Alagu would go out of the village, he put the same responsibility on Jumman. They did not dine together because of the difference in their religion, but their thoughts synched and that indeed was the secret of their friendship.

This friendship started when both of them were still kids and Jumrati, Jumman's father, used to teach them. Alagu had served his teacher well. He had washed many a plate and many a cup. He never let Jumrati's hukkah lay idle, primarily because each fill would allow Alagu to remain away from books at least for half an hour. Alagu's father was a man of conventional thoughts. He believed in the service of the teacher rather than in schooling. He used to say that study has no relation to knowledge; everything is gifted by the grace of the teacher. One should only have the blessings of the teacher. Therefore, even after the support and guidance of Jumrati Sheikh if there was no change in Alagu, he was contented with the thought that he did his best to gain an education but it was not in his fate.

However, Jumrati Sheikh, himself, did not believe much in such blessings. He had more faith in his cane; and due to enlightened use of that stick, Jumman Sheikh was much on call in the nearby villages. Even the clerks of the court could not put a finger on a sale deed or an agreement for a mortgage scripted by Jumman Sheikh. The postman, constable of the area and peon of the district all wanted to be in his good books. Therefore if Alagu was respected for his wealth, Jumman Sheikh was honoured for his valuable knowledge.

2

There was an old maternal aunt of Jumman Sheikh. She possessed a small property, but she had no heir in immediate relations. Jumman had got that property transferred in his name by promising to look after her properly. Till the property was not registered in Jumman's name, the aunt was treated with kindness; she was given all the good things. But as soon as the deed was finalised, her luxuries ended. Jumman's wife, Kariman now started giving some bitter insults to chew along with the chapatis. Jumman Sheikh also became unsympathetic. Now the unfortunate old woman had to tolerate these insults on a daily basis.

'God knows how many more years this ugly old woman would live! She has given us two-three bighas[27] of empty land and she believes that she has bought us! She won't have chapatis without pulses! The amount we have spent on feeding her would have bought us a village!'

For some days the old woman tolerated the invectives but when she could not forgo it anymore, she ran down to Jumman. Jumman didn't think it right to intervene in the

---

27. A land measurement unit prevelant in North India. 1 bigha is 27,000 in square feet.

authority of his wife. Some more days went by like this. Then one day his aunt complained to Jumman— 'Son! I cannot stay anymore in this house. You should give me a monthly income from my land, and I shall bear my expenses with that.'

Jumman said rashly, 'You are saying as if money grows on trees!'

The aunt gently replied, 'Don't I need something to maintain myself?'

Jumman retorted in a serious tone, 'Who knew that you could escape death for so long?'

The aunt was furious, she threatened she would assemble the village council. Jumman smirked just as a trapper would when he sees a deer going toward his trap. He said, 'Yes, you should summon the village council. This matter should be resolved after all. I am fed up with this daily nuisance.'

Jumman had no doubt about who would triumph in the council. There was nobody in the nearby villages, who had not taken his services; who would dare to make him their enemy? Who had the strength to fight against him? And obviously, no angels from heaven would descend to sit for the village council.

3

For many days, the old woman went around in the nearby villages with her walking stick. Her back was lowered like a bow. She took each of her steps with great uneasiness, but it was a matter of justice. It was crucial to come to a decision.

There was barely a person left to whom the old woman did not cry her story. Some would apparently agree with her, others would simply curse the times. Some said—'You are about to die after all. What do you require the property for? You should feed yourself with whatever you get and pass your days in praises of God!' Some also found this a laughing matter and mocked her. After all, a lowered back, a sunken mouth and white hair, all combined, are meant to sprout laughter. There were very few just, kind and sympathetic folks who heard her and consoled her. Finally, she reached Alagu Chaudhary. She put her stick down, took a breath and said, 'Son, it would be nice if you too could make it to my village council for some time.'

Alagu - 'What is the point of calling me? Many people will come from the village.'

The aunt - 'I have told my misfortunes to everyone. To come or not is their choice.'

Alagu - 'I shall come, but will not utter anything in the council.'

The aunt - 'Why is that son?'

Alagu - 'What should I answer to that? It is my choice. Jumman is an old friend. I cannot be against him.'

The aunt - 'Son, will you sacrifice honesty for the fear of a rift?'

Our inner soul does not sense that it is being ruined, but when somebody appeals to it, it becomes conscious. Then it becomes unconquerable. Alagu had no answer to this question, but his heart was ringing with the words—will you sacrifice honesty for the fear of a rift?

4

In the evening, the village council assembled under a tree. Jumman Sheikh had already reached the area and floored the carpet. He had also made arrangements for paan[28], cardamom, narghile and tobacco. He was seated at a distance

---

28. Betel quid, a treat that consists of an areca leaf usually filled with chopped areca nut, slaked lime and a red paste made from the khair tree.

from Alagu Chaudhary and would greet anybody who joined the gathering. As the sun set and the birds came back to the trees to chatter, and here the council began. Every inch of the carpet was occupied, but most of them were only spectators. Among the invited, only those came who wanted to settle their scores with Jumman for something or the other. A fire was burning in a corner. A barber was speedily filling chillams. It was difficult to ascertain what caused more smoke, the burning dung-cakes or the chillams. The boys were running around headlong. Some would quarrel and others would cry. There was a hubbub all around. Groups of dogs had arrived mistaking this gathering for some sort of a feast.

When the jury[29] settled down, the old aunt entreated them 'Jury, three years have passed since I relinquished my property in favour of my nephew Jumman. You know him very well. Jumman promised to look after me until I die. I somehow spent a year in misery with him. But I cannot live with him anymore. Neither do I get the required food to maintain myself, nor do I get sufficient clothes to cover my body. I am a helpless widow. I cannot go and file a court case. Who else should I appeal to except you? I shall follow whatever you decide. If you see any error on my part, you are free to penalise me. If you see any shortcomings in Jumman's behaviour, advise him to be generous to a helpless woman. I shall respect your decision without question.'

Ramdhan Mishra, many of whose tenants Jumman had settled in his village, said, 'Jumman, whom do you choose as the judge of your case? Decide on this now. You shall then have to abide by whatever is decided by him.'

---

29. Jury comprises of persons that are to be addressed as 'Panch' in Hindi. Usually they are the seniormost dwellers of the village. The judge of a case is chosen by the parties with mutual consent from among the jury members.

Jumman, at this time, could see only those people in the assembly who had some grudge against him. Jumman answered, 'The decision of the judge is the decision of God himself. My dear aunt can appoint anybody she wants. I do not have any objection.'

The aunt yelled, 'For the love of God, why don't you decide the name of your appointee? I wish to know whom you want to appoint.'

'Don't force me to speak the truth now! Everybody here is on your side. Choose whomsoever you wish!', Jumman said irefully.

The Aunt understood Jumman's indictments and said, 'Son, fear the God! The jury is impartial, they are nobody's friend or fiend. What are you even saying? But even if you do not believe anybody else, you believe in Alagu Chaudhary, right? Here, I nominate Alagu Chaudhary as the judge.'

Jumman Sheikh was delighted, but concealing his feelings he said, 'As you say, let it be Alagu. For me, Alagu or Ramdhan, they are both the same.'

Alagu did not want to be a part of this dispute. He tried avoiding it and said, 'Aunt, you know Jumman and I are very close friends.'

The aunt retorted with gravity, 'Son, a man does not abandon his morality for friendship. God himself resides in the heart of a jury member. Whatever they say is the command of God himself.'

Alagu Chaudhary was nominated as the judge for this case; Ramdhan Mishra and other foes of Jumman cursed the old woman in their hearts.

Alagu Chaudhary said, 'Sheikh Jumman, we are old friends. When I was in need, you helped me and I have returned in kind. But right now, you and your old aunt are alike in my eyes. You can tell us your side now.'

Jumman was sure in his heart—'Now, I will win the case. Alagu is only saying all these things superficially; he does not mean it.' Therefore he calmly answered 'Jury, it has been three years since my dear aunt transferred her property in my name. I had agreed to take care of donning and feeding her until the day she lives. God knows, I never troubled her for anything. I respected her as I respect my own mother. To serve her is my responsibility; but when the ladies in the household fight, I am helpless. Now, my dear aunt is asking me for monthly stipends. You all know how much property it is. It does not produce enough profit even to fund her expenses. Apart from that, there is nothing written about monthly charges in the agreement; I would not have pledged myself to it if it were so. I do not have to say anything else. The council has the right to decide my case in whichever manner they deem fit.'

Alagu Chaudhary was well acquainted with the ways of law and courts. He started interrogating Jumman. Each question was a blow to Jumman's heart. Ramdhan Mishra was amused by every question. Jumman was shocked— 'Just a moment ago this very same Alagu was sitting by my side and talking affably. In this little time, he has taken such a 180 degrees turn that he is now digging my grave. What has happened to him? What long-forgotten score is he trying to settle between us? Will our friendship of so many years be of no use?'

Jumman Sheikh was still lost in his thoughts when Alagu announced the judgement—'Jumman Sheikh! The council has looked into this case. We consider, in accordance with justice, that the aunt shall be given monthly stipends. We believe that her property brings about enough profit to manage her monthly expenses. This is our decision. If Jumman does not consent to pay the expenses, the agreement shall be considered null and void.'

Jumman was stunned at this decision. If your friend starts behaving like your enemy and holds a knife to your throat, what will you call it except that the times have now changed? A friend that I trusted the most deceived me when I needed him the most. It is only at times like these that one can tell a false friend from a true one. This is the friendship of corrupt times. Had people not been this false and deceiving, our country would not have ached from so many troubles. Certainly, this cholera, plague, etc. are the karma of such evils.

But Ramdhan Mishra and the other jury members were admiring and singing praises of Alagu Chaudhary's impartiality and sense of justice. They said, 'This is what a village council is! It brings out the truth. Friendship has its own place, but it is important to perform one's duty. Only due to such just men, the world still exists!'

This decision shook the roots of their friendship. Now Jumman and Alagu were not seen talking to each other like before. They had nourished this friendship like a tree over many years, but even such an old tree could not stand a minor gust of truth. It was surely standing on sandy ground. Now formality began to supersede their behaviour with each other. Their courtesies to each other increased. Both continued to meet, but their togetherness was akin to the meeting of sword and shield.

Jumman was burning with revenge. The deemed betrayal by his friend gripped his thoughts day and night.

5

Good things take a long time to transpire, but the same is not true for bad ones; Jumman also got the opportunity to take his revenge shortly. The previous year, Alagu Chaudhary had purchased a first-class pair of oxen from Batesar. The oxen were of the topmost breed; sturdy with big horns. For months people from close-by areas would come just to have a look at them. Unfortunately, one amongst the pair died a month after the council of Jumman. Jumman said to his friends— 'This is the punishment for deceiving. Man perhaps may not do anything, but God sees everything and acts accordingly.' Alagu suspected that Jumman has caused his ox to be poisoned. His wife also blamed Jumman and declared him responsible. One day a tiff arose between her and Kariman on the subject. Both the ladies crossed words furiously. The exchange of words was decked with sarcasm, quibbles, euphemisms, allegories etc. Jumman somehow ended the squabble. He rebuked and stopped his wife and brought her home from that battlefield. Here, Alagu Chaudhary used his stick to put sense into his wife.

Now, what would a single ox do? Alagu searched a lot for a suitable ox to pair him with but could not find one. The only option that remained was to sell him. Samjhu Sahu in the village used to ride an ekka cart[30]. He would take stacks of jaggary and ghee from the village to the market and return with oil, salt, etc. from there to sell in the village. He eyed this ox. He thought—'If I bought this ox, I can clearly make three rounds in a day. Presently, I rarely take one round.' He inspected the ox, took him for a test ride with his cart, examined if he will bode well, bargained and finally got it home. He guaranteed to pay for him within one month. Chaudhary also wanted to sell him after all, so he did not care for the loss.

---

30. A cart drawn by a single animal.

Samjhu Sahu got the new ox and began to take substantial work from him. He arranged to make three rounds a day, sometimes even four. He did not provide for forage or water; his aim was to take as many rounds as possible a day. He would carry the ox to the market and feed him some dry hay. The poor animal could hardly relax and would again be tied to the cart. In Alagu's home, he had a tranquil and untroubled life. He would only occasionally be used in the passenger cart. He would have clean water, lentils, and pomace with hay; and as if that was not enough, sometimes he would even relish ghee. A person would rub him two times a day. The condition here was entirely the opposite; the ox had to work all day long. In a month he became a shadow of his former self; his skeleton could be easily seen through his skin. The glimpse of the ekka would be sufficient for him to panic. Even a step forward was a lot of effort for him.

One day, Sahu piled up double the usual weight in the fourth round to home. The animal was exceptionally tired, but Sahu started to whip it. The ox summoned all his reserve of power and started to walk. It ran for some time and then stopped to relax for a moment, but Sahu wanted to get home soon so he lashed the ox repeatedly. The ox tried one more time, but this time his muscles gave up and it fell to the ground. Sahu tried to pull it by its legs and even put a stick up its nose; but how could a dead ox get up? Sahu looked at it firmly, untied the cart and begin to think of a method to bring the cart home. He called out in a loud voice; but the village roads are shut as soon as it is evening, just like the children's eyes. He saw nobody and there was no village close by. He kicked the ox once again in anger and started abusing it— 'If only it would die after getting home! The wretch died in between! Now how would the cart get back home?' In this way, Sahu murmured a lot. He had sold many sacks of jaggary and many drums of ghee and its proceeds, about two hundred rupees, were kept in his waist. Apart from that, there were many sacks of salt on the cart and canisters of oil; so the cart could not be left either. Seeing no other option, he decided to spend the night there guarding the cart. He sang, smoked and kept himself awake till midnight and then unknowingly fell asleep. When he got up in the morning and checked his waist, his purse was not there! Trembling badly, he looked into his cart and found that many canisters of oil had been taken away. He came home in this miserable state. When his wife heard the story, at first she stopped shocked and then started to criticise Alagu Chaudhary— 'The rascal gave such an unfortunate ox that our life's savings are gone.'

Many months went by. Whenever Alagu would talk about the payment for his ox, Sahu would attack him with irritatable words— 'Here we have lost our entire earnings and this person wants us to pay for that! You gave us an almost dead ox and now you come asking for money! You tricked us, gave us such a futile ox! Do you think we are idiots? We are traders, not fools! Firstly, you should not even ask for the money but even if you do, we allow you to take our ox and use it not for one but two months. That should make the deal even!'

There was no dearth of Chaudhary's enemies. In such situations, they too would take Sahu's side. But it was not simple to forgo one hundred fifty rupees. So once he asked for the money firmly. Sahu also became furious and the quarrel turned into an ugly fight. Finally, some intelligent people from the village came out of their homes and asked them to sit for a village council and accept its judgement. Sahu and Alagu both agreed to the advice.

6

The village council was about to be called in a few days. Both parties began pulling people to their sides and on the third day, the council sat under the same tree. It was evening. Crows were having their own council to discuss whether they have any claim on the peas that were ready in the fields, and until the matter was solved they deemed it their duty to show their disliking at the call of their caretaker. The parrots sitting on the branches of the tree were conferring whether the humans had any right to call them heedless when they themselves did not bash up from cheating their friends.

When the council began, Ramdhan Mishra said, 'Without waiting we should select the judge. Chaudhary, whom do you want as the judge?'

Alagu said gently 'Let Samjhu Sahu choose.'

Samjhu got up quickly and confidently said 'Jumman Sheikh from my side!'

As soon as Alagu heard Jumman's name, his heart began to beat violently; he felt as if somebody has slapped him hard. Ramdhan was a friend of Alagu; he soon guessed the matter and asked 'Chaudhary, do you have any disagreement?'

Chaudhary said dejectedly, 'No, why would there be any disagreement?'

The consciousness of responsibility usually rectifies our trifling conduct. When we start to stray from our way, this awareness guides us back to the path. An editor, resting in his cabin attacks the ministers with his brave pen using harsh words; but such situations come when an editor becomes a minister. As soon as he gets a ministerial position, his pen becomes sensitive, thoughtful and balanced. The reason for that is the consciousness of responsibility. How arrogant a young man is during his teenage. His parents are always concerned for him. They think of him as a smear on their good name. But as soon as the responsibility of his family begins to fall on his shoulders, the same impatient, careless youth is converted into a patient and responsible man; this too is the outcome of the realisation of responsibilities.

As soon as Jumman Sheikh became the judge, he became aware of this sense of responsibility. He thought—'Right now I am holding the highest throne of justice. Whatever I utter now is parallel to God's own word, and God's word can surely not be soiled by my shallow thinking. It is not okay to even divert a little from the truth!'

The jury began to question both parties. For a long time, both parties kept contending for their sides. All of them were of the opinion that Samjhu should pay for the ox. But there were two men who wanted some relaxation for Samjhu as he had undergone loss due to the ox's death. In opposition to that, two men not only anted Samjhu to pay for the ox but also wanted to punish him so that no man ever would treat animals with such cruelty. In the end, Jumman declared— 'Alagu Chaudhary and Samjhu Sahu! The council has carefully looked into your case. It is legal for Samjhu to pay the full price of the ox. When he bought it, it was healthy. If he had paid for it right then, all this matter would not have come up. The ox died just because it was overloaded with work without enough arrangements for its feed.'

Ramdhan Mishra said, 'Samjhu has deliberately killed the ox, so he should be punished.'

Jumman said, 'This is another matter, separate from the one under consideration!'

Jhagdu Sahu said, 'Samjhu should be given some relaxation.'

Jumman said, 'That is entirely on Alagu Chaudhary. He can do it out of his kindness.'

Alagu Chaudhary was out of the world with happiness. He stood up and exclaimed loudly, 'Hail the jury!'

Declarations came from all around 'Hail the jury!'

Everyone admired Jumman's just decision— 'This is what justice is! This is not the work of humans, God himself voiced through the jury; it is His justice! Who can fake before the jury?

After a while Jumman came to Alagu and embracing him said— 'Brother, since the day you gave the decision in the village council, I had become your deadly enemy; but today I got to know that when sitting as a jury you are nobody's friend or enemy. One cannot think of anything but justice then. Today I accept that the word of the jury is the word of God.' Alagu started crying. This water cleared all the smut in their hearts. The scorched vine of their friendship became green again.

9. The Aged Aunt

1

Old age, in many ways, is said to be the return of childhood. The aged aunt had lost all her senses except that of taste, and she had no other means to draw attention to her ailments except crying. All her senses—eyes, hands and legs—had given up. She would lie on the floor and, if the members of the family did things against her wishes, not give her food on time or not in enough quantity, or if something came into the house and was not given to her, she would begin to cry aloud. Her crying was not in the least manner usual or normal. She would always whine and wail aloud.

A long time had passed since her husband had died. Her son, too, had died in his adolescence. And now, there was no one except the nephew with whom she lived. She had written her entire property in his name. The nephew had made big promises at the time, but they came out to be false. The yearly income from her property was not less than one hundred and fifty rupees, but she was scarcely given enough to keep her belly full. It was not clear whether her nephew, Pandit Buddhiram, was responsible for this, or his wife. Buddhiram was a decent gentleman, but only as long as he did not have to hand over his money. Rupa was sharp by nature but God-fearing. The aged aunt did not mind her sharp tongue as much as she did Buddhiram's apparent refined behaviour.

Sometimes Buddhiram repented his callous behaviour. He understood very well that he could act like a gentleman because of this property. If verbal assurances and dry sympathy could improve his situation, he would not mind it at all. But the fear of extra costs made him vanquish all his good thinking. If the old aunt communicated her troubles with a visitor, he would go into a rage and scold the aunt. Children usually dislike old people. When they saw the behaviour of their parents towards her, they mocked her all the more. Someone pinched her; another would spill water on her after cleaning. If the aunt would let out a yell, everyone presumed that she cried and yelled only for food, no one paid any notice. Now if the aunt, in a state of anger, started cursing the children, Rupa would be there all watchful. This fear made the aunt use her tongue as a weapon scarcely, though it certainly was a more powerful weapon than crying to get her needs.

In the whole family, if the aunt was close to anyone, it was Ladli, Buddhiram's youngest daughter. Fearing her ravaged brothers, Ladli would take her portion of sweets to the aged aunt's room and eat them there. This was her shelter, though it sometimes came out to be rather costly because of the aunt's greed, yet low-priced than her brothers' injustice. Their self-interest had aroused sympathy between them.

2

It was night. A shehnai[31] was playing in Buddhiram's courtyard, and the children of the village were enjoying the music with google-eyed wonder. The guests were resting on cots and getting massaged by the barber. The village minstrel was standing there and singing and, flipped away by this, some guests were yelling 'Bravo! Bravo!' The singer

---

31. A musical instrument.

looked elated, as though he really deserved the praise. Some English-educated youths were there who did not care for it. They considered it low for their dignity to be a part of the assembly of fools.

The occasion was Buddhiram's eldest son, Sukhram's tilak ceremony[32]. People had gathered there to commemorate it. Women were singing inside the house, and Rupa was busy with the arrangements for the feast. Huge pans were put on the earthen baker. If puris and kachoris were being fried in one, other dishes were being prepared in others. Spicy curries were being cooked in another huge pan. The appetizing odour of ghee and spices had filled the place.

The aunt was lying in her room, dejected. The spicy aroma was making her edgy. She was thinking, *they won't part me any puris, I guess. It's so late, but no one has brought me anything to eat. It seems everyone has been fed. Nothing has remained for me.* This made her feel like howling, but she restrained thinking that such actions will not be appropriate on such a pious event.

Ah! What aroma! Who'll think of me? When they don't give me sufficient rotis, will they give me delicious puris? With this thought, tears rolled down her eyes and she felt a lump in her throat. But she remained silent for fear of Rupa.

The aunt was lost in such sorrowful thoughts for a while now. The fragrance of ghee and spices continued to make her restless. Her mouth was watering. The thought of the taste of the puris tickled her inside. Whom should I call? Even Ladli is not here today. The two boys who always poked me are also nowhere around. No one knew where they had vanished today. I should get to know what is being cooked today.

---

32. One of the rituals in a Hindu wedding of North India.

The aged aunt's imagination flew as she thought of the puris spinning before her eyes. Deep red, fluffed up and soft to touch puris. Rupa must have dined to her heart's fill. The kachoris must be releasing the aroma of *ajwain* and cardamom. If she could just touch a puri with her hands, she would love it. She felt like visiting the scene and sitting in front of the pan. The puris must be rolling out of the pan. They must be bringing them out of the pan and serving them hot. One can smell flowers in the house, but it is altogether a different experience to smell them in the garden. Having confirmed, the aunt sat on all fours and, down on her hands, got out of the threshold with difficulty and quietly crawled to the pan.

At that time Rupa was busy carrying out her duties. Now she went inside one room, then another; at times she would go near the pan and the next second to the place where the food was being kept. Someone came from the door and said, 'Maharaj is demanding a milkshake.' She became busy handing him a milkshake. The next moment someone else arrived and said, 'The village minstrel is here, give him something.' She was taking out a share for the minstrel when a third person appeared and asked, 'in how much time the dinner would be ready? Could you hand me the drum and the cymbals?' Poor thing, she was tired from running around and she felt angry too, but she had no time to express her annoyance. If she poured out her anger, her neighbours would mock her saying she had no potential to manage even an occasion. Her throat was bone dry because of thirst. She was burning in the heat. But she didn't have the time either to have water or fan herself. She was also anxious about the fact that if she was not there or there was the slightest laxity on her part then things would begin to run down. In this mental state when she saw the aged aunt sitting near the pan, she flared up. She could not control herself. She forgot about her fellow neighbours who were sitting there and did not care what they would think if they saw her rebuking the old woman. Similar to a frog who jumps on a snail, she pounced on the aunt, shook her by the arms and said, 'Is your stomach on fire already? Is it a belly or a warehouse? Couldn't you sit still in your room? The guests have not been served yet, offerings to God have not been made—couldn't you wait for some time more? You have come out to sit on my chest. May God burn your tongue. If you aren't given food the whole day, you will go out attacking other people's kitchens. The village people will think that you are not provided with sufficient food in the house: that is why you look for food elsewhere. She doesn't even die, this witch! She is determined in soiling our honour. She will stop only when we lose our reputation in society. She feeds herself with so much; I don't know how she burns it off. If you care for your life, be inside your room and sit there; when the people in the family will sit down to eat, you will get your food. You are not a goddess that you should be worshipped first, never mind if no one else has taken even a drop of water.'

The aged aunt put up her head; she did not cry or say anything. Quietly she brought herself back to her room. Rupa's tone was so rude that her entire mind, senses and all her feelings marched towards it. When a big tree from the riverbank falls into the river, water from around rushes to fill the gap made by it!

3

The feast was ready. Leaf plates were laid out, and the guests began to eat. The women sang songs. The barber and other servants who came with the guests also sat down to eat a little far from the group, but as a matter of manners no one could stand up before everyone had their fill. One or two guests who were somewhat literate were uncomfortable because the servants were taking too much time. They believed this limitation to be useless and irrational.

Sitting in her room, the aged aunt was agonizing over the words that had brought her so much disgrace. She was not furious with Rupa but cursing herself for her own agitation. *She was saying the truth—how can the family members eat before the guests? I could not show this much patience and had to face humiliation before everyone. Now, I won't go as long as I'm not called.*

Thinking this, she began to wait for the call. But the tasteful environment of ghee was testing her patience. Every moment passed like an age to her. *Now the plates must have been laid out! The guests must have arrived. People must be washing their hands and feet, the barber must be serving water.* She imagined that people must have sat down to eat. The songs were still on; she lay down to take rest and began to hum a song. Now she felt that she had been singing for long. Were the guests still dining? She could not hear any sound. *People must have gone after the feast. No one came to see me. Rupa is furious, she might not call me. She must be thinking that I will come on my own. After all, I was not a guest that she should come to invite me.* The old aunt managed to bring herself out. The prediction that she would have puris and spicy curry tickled her senses. She began making all kinds of plans in her mind. *First, I will eat the puris with vegetable curry, then with curd and sugar. The kachoris will taste better with raita. I will call for several servings, never mind what people might say. They might think that I have no control over myself. Let them. I am going to eat puris after such a long time and can't be contented without having my fill.* She moved down to the courtyard and sat on all fours. But fate was not with her again. Her uncontrollable mind had miscalculated the time, the guests were still sitting. Some had just finished eating and were tasting their fingers; some looked from the side of their eyes to see if others were still eating. Some were fretting about how to take the remaining puris with them. Some had finished the curd but were longing for a second serving for which they were hesitating to ask. In this, the aunt slowly crawled between the guests. Several men got up, frightened. They yelled, 'Who is this old woman? Where has she come from? Take care that she doesn't get close to you.'

Buddhiram was enraged at the sight of the aunt. He had a plate of puris. He threw the plate to the ground and, just as a rude moneylender jumps on an unfaithful and fugitive borrower, he held the aunt with both hands, dragged her to the dark room and flung her inside. The aunt's fantasy was destroyed in a moment by the blow of a tornado.

The guests finished eating. The family members also ate. The musicians, the washerman and the cobbler, too, had dined. But no one recalled the aunt. Both Buddhiram and Rupa had decided to punish her for her shamelessness. No one took pity on her old age, her fate and her helplessness, except Ladli who was in pain for her grandmother.

Ladli was deeply attached to the aged aunt. An innocent and simple-hearted girl, she had no trace of childish humour or playfulness. On both occasions when her parents had dragged the aunt away with such cruelty, Ladli's heart cried for her. She was annoyed that her parents did not immediately give the aunt a lot of puris. Would the guests eat all of them? And would the earth fall if aunt ate before the guests? She wanted to go to the aunt to console her but could not for fear of her mother. She had not eaten her part of puris at all, but had kept them hidden in the doll box. She wanted to take them to her and was growing uneasy. *Hearing my footsteps aunt will get up and be so happy seeing the puris. She will bestow her love on me.*

4

It was eleven at night. Rupa was sleeping in the courtyard. But Ladli's eyes could not give themselves any rest. The urge to see the aunt's happiness while eating *puris* did not let her sleep. The doll box was right there in front of her. When she felt that her mother had fallen asleep she got up and wanted to go to the aunt. But it was pitch dark outside. Only the ashes in the earthen ovens were still lit, and a dog was resting there. Her eyes fell towards the neem tree beside the door. She assumed as though Hanumanji was sitting on it. She could see his tail and stick quite clearly. She closed her eyes in fear. At that moment the dog sat up, and this gave strength to Ladli. A waking dog provided her more security than sleeping human beings. She lifted the box and made for the aunt's room.

5

The aunt could only remember that someone had held her by the hand and dragged her along. Then it felt as though someone was flying her to a mountain. Her feet hit stones again and again and then someone threw her down from the mountain and she died.

Now that she had regained her senses, there was silence everywhere. She assumed that everyone must have eaten and gone to sleep, and with them, her fate had also gone to sleep. Oh God, how could she pass the night without food? A fire was burning in her belly. *Ah! No one gave a thought to me. Will they raise their wealth by cutting down on my food? These people do not show any worry that this old woman might die any day. Why hurt her? I just eat a couple of rotis and nothing more and for this such is the condition. I am a blind and handicapped woman—I don't hear or understand anything. Even if I had gone to the courtyard Buddhiram could have told me that aunt the guests are eating right now, you can come after some time. He dragged me and then dumped me here. Rupa abused me in front of everyone for the puris. Even after doing all this to me, their iron hearts did not melt. They fed everyone but did not come to ask me. If they didn't give me anything then, how will they give now?*

Thinking thus, the aunt lay down, resigned to her fate. The humiliation hurt her deeply and she had wanted to cry her heart out, but she could not do so as the guests were there.

Instantly, she heard someone saying, 'Aunt, get up. I have got puris.' The aunt identified Ladli's voice. She sat up with eagerness. She fished for Ladli with both her hands and got her to sit on her knees. Ladli took out the puris and offered them to her.

The aunt asked, 'Did your Amma allow them?'

Ladli replied, 'No. It's my share.'

The aunt held the puris. She emptied the box in five minutes.

Ladli asked, 'Aunt, did you have your suffice?'

Just as a few drops of rain rises the temperature up instead of lowering it down, these few puris aroused the aunt's craving and hunger further. She said, 'No, girl. Go to your mother and bring some more.'

Ladli answered, 'Amma is sleeping. If I wake her up, she'll beat me.'

The aunt perused the box once again. There lay some leftover pieces that she picked and ate. She licked her lips, again and again, hungering for more.

The aunt's heart was craving more and more puris. When the line of satisfaction breaks then one's thirst crosses all limits. If drunkards are reminded of alcohol, they are blinded by their desire for it. The aunt's impatient mind was carried away by the strong current of her desire. She forgot the difference between right and wrong. She got hold of her desire for some time, and then suddenly said to Ladli, 'Hold my hand and lead me to the place where the guests were eating.'

Ladli couldn't guess what was going on in her mind. She took her hand and took her to the place which was now packed with used leaf plates in which people had eaten their food. The miserable hungry woman started to pick leftover pieces of puris from the leaf plates and eat them. How tasty was the curd! How delicious the kachoris! And how soft the *khasta!* However dimwitted she might have been, she understood very well that she was doing something she should not do. *I'm licking empty plates thrown by others!* But old age is the last stage when all our desires get to a single point. In the aged aunt's case, this centre was her sense of taste.

Just at that moment, Rupa got up and realised that Ladli was not there by her side. She became concerned and looked around the cot, maybe Ladli had tumbled off from it. When she didn't find her, she came out to see her standing beside the used leaf plates, while the old aunt was eating pieces of leftover puris from them. Rupa was shocked by the sight. Her state at that moment was like the feeling of a cow that sees its own throat being cut. What can be a more painful sight than a Brahmin woman searching for food in leftovers? For some pieces of puris her mother-in-law was resorting to such a lowly and deplorable act! It was a scene that would shock anyone. It seemed as though the earth had fixed on its axis and the sky was rolling around, that a crisis was going to strike the world. Rupa didn't feel furious. Her anger melted into deep sorrow. Shame and fear rolled tears down her eyes. Who was to blame for this *adharma?* She raised her hands towards the heavens and said with a pure heart, 'My God. Have compassion for my children. Do not punish me for this adharma. I'll be finished.'

Rupa had never seen an exhibition of her own selfishness and injustice manifest itself before. She thought, *how cruel can I be? I have reduced and brought someone to this state from whose property I get an income of two hundred rupees per year! It is all my actions. Oh, merciful God! I've committed a sin. Please forgive me. It was my son's tilak ceremony today. Hundreds of people were fed. I was a slave to their wishes. We spent hundreds of rupees on our reputation. But the one whose money helped us do this was left starving. Just because that old woman cannot help herself!*

Rupa lit the lamp, opened the door of the dresser, arranged all the food on a plate and moved towards the aunt's room.

It was past midnight. The sky looked like a large plate of stars on which the angels were decorating heavenly offerings. But none of them could experience the extreme joy that the aunt felt when she saw the plate in front of her. Rupa said with a choked voice, 'Aunt, get up. Have your meal. Please forgive me for my shortcomings today. Pray to God that He may forgo my crime.'

Like simple, innocent children who forget the chiding and beating of their mother the moment she gives them sweets, the aged aunt began to eat, oblivious of everything else. Every part of her body released a blessing for Rupa who was lost in that moment of heavenly bliss.

10. A Grave Problem

1

In my office there were four peons, one of whom was Garib. He was exceptionally simple, dutiful, alert, an efficient worker and one who would take any criticism without any complain—the name 'Garib[33]' and his personality go well together in his case. I have been in this office for a year and never found him away from work. I am so used to seeing him sitting on his worn-out mat at nine in the morning, as if he were an intrinsic part of the office building. So innocent is he that he cannot say no to anyone or anything.

There's another peon, a Muslim. The whole office is scared of him, one wonders why. I cannot think of anything in his case but that he is boisterous. He boasts of having a cousin who is a *qazi*[34] in the state of Rampur and an uncle who is a magistrate in the state of Tonk. Our office has conferred on him the title of 'Qazi Sahib'.

The remaining two come from the brahmin caste[35]. People rate their blessings higher than the duties they may perform. Both are shirkers, arrogant and lazy. You ask them to do something and they make faces before carrying

---

33. 'Garib' in Hindi language means a poor man.
34. Magistrate or judge of a Islamic religious court.
35. Considered upper caste as per the heirarchy of Hindu social system.

it out. They damn care for the clerks. Only the head of the office has some importance, but sometimes they mess with him, too.

Amidst all this, no one is treated as badly as poor Garib. When it's time to get a promotion, the three benefit themselves of it; no one thinks of Garib. All three have risen to ten rupees a month, yet Garib is stuck at seven. From morning till evening, he is on his feet—even the three fellow peons order him around. They also make additional income from tips, which is not shared with him. On top of this, everyone in the office—from the diarist to the head clerk—has a grouse against him. There have been endless complaints against him and many a time he has been fined too, in addition to the regular reprimandations. I never understood the mystery behind this. I did sympathize with him and also showed that his place in my heart was not lower than that of the others. On a few occasions, I have fought with others in his favour.

<h2 style="text-align:center">2</h2>

One day, the office head asked Garib to clean his table. Immediately, he set to it. Accidentally, the duster touched the inkpot and it tumbled, the ink spilling all over the table. The head was furious. He got hold of Garib by the ear and showered him with abuses from all popular languages spoken in India.

Poor Garib! He stood still with tears in his eyes as if he had committed murder. I didn't like this brutal, unbearable conduct of the head. If another peon had done something even worse, the head would not have behaved in this manner. I said to him in English, 'Sir, this is highly unjust. He didn't spill the ink intentionally. This extreme punishment is the limit of impropriety.'

The head politely said, 'You do not know him. He is very wicked.'

'I do not find him wicked.'

'You do not know him yet, sir. He's one of a kind. He has two ploughs for the fields, he deals in thousands, has many buffaloes. This has made him arrogant.'

'If that were the case, why would he be a peon here?'

'Believe me, the fellow is loaded but is a total scrooge.'

'This is no crime, is it?'

'You are not aware of these things yet. Wait for some more time and you will realize how cheap and small he is.'

Another one from the office butted in, 'Sir, he had tonnes of milk and curd at home, tonnes of peas, maize and gram. Yet he has never thought of giving even a little to the people in the office. We pine for these things here. Why shouldn't we be jealous? And all his prosperity is due to his present job. Earlier, he didn't even have a morsel to eat.'

The head said hesitatingly, 'That's not the issue. It's all his and it is up to him if he wants to give it to others. Yet, the fellow is inconsiderate, an animal.'

I grasped the matter quickly and said, 'If he's so small a person, then he is an animal. I didn't realize this.'

The head opened up more now. His hesitation was also gone. He said, 'Not that his gifts will change anything for others, but they surely will reveal his good-natured heart. One doesn't expect anything from a poor man. What can one take from a starving man?

The secret was out. The head had shown the entire situation in the simplest manner. A prosperous man has many enemies, big shots and even the modest. If our in-laws or if our mother's paternal side is not well-off we do not expect anything from them. But, if they are prosperous and yet do care for us on festivities, we get jealous. When we go to a poor friend's house, we remain satisfied with a plain betel leaf. But tell me a person who will not curse and be furious with a prosperous friend for life if he does not offer us a proper meal? If poor Sudama had come empty-handed from Lord Krishna's, he would have considered him a worse enemy than Shishupal and Jarasandh. This is human nature.

3

A few days later, I asked Garib, 'Tell me, do you plough your fields?'

Garib said modestly, 'Yes, sir, I do. I have two labourers who work in the fields.'

'You have cows and buffaloes too?'

'Yes, sir, I have two milk-giving buffaloes. The cow is pregnant. It's because of people's generosity that I manage to have two square meals a day.'

'Do you ever give some alms to us government officials?'

Garib replied with humility, 'What do I have to give to them, sir? What does my land give but barley, gram, maize and sorghum? You are all kings, how can I give you such miserly things. I am afraid that I'd be scolded that how does he have the nerve to do this? That is the reason, sir, I dare not. Milk and curd are not worth offering. Anything I give should at least be worth them, sir.'

'Bring something someday, see what people say. Such things are hardly available in the cities. These people yearn for such miserly things sometimes.'

'Sir, what if someone takes offence? What if they complain about me? I will not be able to show my face.'

'Leave that to me. Nobody will say anything to you. If anybody will say something, I'll explain it to them.'

'Well, sir, these days peas are growing. Gram is also sprouting. The cane crusher has opened. There's nothing more, sir!'

'Just bring these.'

'If things go south, you will have to save me.'

'Yes, I have told you, it is my responsibility.'

The next day Garib came to the office, with three young sturdy men. Two had baskets filled with pods of green peas on their head. One had an earthen jar on his head full of sugarcane juice. All three of them carried bundles of sugarcane, held under their underarms. Garib silently came and stood under a tree in front of the veranda. He was afraid of entering the office as if he was a criminal. Just then some peons and other officials came and cornered him. One chewed on the sugarcane, some others pounced on the basket; pillaging had begun. Meanwhile, the head clerk entered the office. On seeing this mayhem, he roared, 'What's all this? Come inside and get back to your work.'

I went to him and whispered, 'Garib has brought all these presents from home. You take some and distribute the remaining amongst others.'

Feigning anger, the head asked, 'Garib, why did you bring these here? Take them away or else I shall lodge a report with the officer. Who do you think we are—beggars?'

Garib paled and shivered with fear. He could not utter a word and only looked at me with expecting eyes.

I apologized to the head on his behalf. After much cajoling, the head was brought around. He sent half the things from each home and the remaining was given to the rest. With this, the great theatrics ended.

4

This incident marked the rise of Garib in the office. Now, no one found faults with him, nor did Garib have to run for tasks. He was spared, too, with the stinging remarks of his colleagues. The other peons would sometimes do his job. His name, too, underwent a change—from Garib, it was changed to Garibdas. This affected his temperament. Self-confidence took the place of forbearance. Also, laziness took place of alertness. He would now sometimes arrive at the office late, on certain days even skip office pretending to be unwell. All his crimes were not forgivable He had found the key to his dignity and prestige. Every week or fortnight, he would get milk, curd, or something else for the head. He had learnt the art of appeasing the gods. His new strength was manipulative skills rather than an innocent way of life.

One day, he was sent by the head to the railway station to get a delivery of parcels coming from the government farms. There were many big bundles. These were transferred through carts. Garib had negotiated with the cart driver and a price of twelve annas for the cartage was settled. When papers were brought to the office, Garib rightly charged twelve annas from the office. His mind changed as soon as he came out. He demanded a share of four annas in payment from the driver. The cart driver was dismayed and declined to part with the sum. Garib angered by this, put the whole amount in his pocket and said rudely, 'you won't be paid a paisa. Go tell whomever you want to.' Noticing that unless he gave his share from their amount, he would not get anything the cart driver agreed. Garib gave him eight annas and asked him to sign on a receipt of twelve annas. Then the receipt was submitted to the office.

This strange scene left me amazed. This was the same Garib who, some months ago, had been an incarnation of humility and honesty, who hadn't had the courage to claim even his own rights from the other peons. He did not know how to bribe others or accept bribes. I was discouraged seeing this change in him. Who was responsible for this change? Yes, I was responsible and I had taught him this low-level manipulation and wickedness. I started thinking— compared to this wickedness that he is willing to grab someone's throat, how was that naivety bad that had made him accept injustices from others in the past? It was an inauspicious moment when I guided this man to the path of gaining dignity for himself. In reality, the path was of his downfall. I had abandoned his self-respect for the sake of him gaining hollow external respect.

11. One-and-a-Quarter Ser[36] of Wheat

1

In a village somewhere, there lived a farmer named, Shankar. He was a poor man who led a simple life and did not interfere in other people's affairs. Since he himself knew no smart moves, he never bothered about being fooled by others. He ate well when he had enough food in the house. When he didn't, he lived on parched gram. When there was no gram either, he drank water, thanked Lord Rama and went to sleep. But when a guest happened to come by, he had to make an exception. And when a sadhu or holy man happened to come at his door, it was a different matter. He could go to sleep hungry himself, but how could he make a sadhu sleep on an empty stomach, for a sadhu was a true follower of God!

One evening a sadhu appeared at Shankar's doorstep. His face radiated a divine light. He was dressed in yellow clothes. His hair was long and knotted. In his hand he carried a brass pot of water, on his feet he wore wooden clogs and spectacles on his eyes. All in all, he looked like the sort of person who showed a keen interest in the prayers of the rich and travelling to devotional spots in aeroplanes as he did in eating good food.

---

36. A unit of dry volume in India. 1 ser is 933.1 grams.

Shankar only had ground barley at home. How could he give that to a sadhu? In olden times, barley may have been considered good, but in the present age, barley is believed to be hard to digest for people of a better class. Poor Shankar was puzzled: What was he to give the holy man to eat? In the end, he decided he must take some wheat flour from someone. But there was no one he could find to borrow some wheat from. After all, it was a village of simple human beings. So how the sadhu's food could be found here? Nevertheless, by great good luck, the village priest had some wheat. Shankar borrowed a quarter and one ser, a bare kilo of wheat, took it home and gave his wife to make it into flour. The sadhu ate well, slept well, gave his blessings and went away early the next morning.

The priest took his share of the harvest twice a year. That very year, Shankar understood that returning one and a quarter ser of wheat was of no use, so instead of the usual five ser he gave the priest, he would give a little extra to settle the account. Shankar assumed the priest would know why the extra sum was being given and the matter would be over. In the harvesting season, when the priest came up to take his share of the harvest, Shankar doubled the usual amount and considered himself free of the burden of debt. However, he made no mention of it and neither did the priest enquire. How was poor Shankar to know that he would have to take rebirth to settle the debt of that one-and-a-quarter ser of wheat!

2

Seven years passed. The priest became a moneylender, and from a farmer, Shankar became a labourer. His younger brother, Mangal, claimed his share of the property and separated. Together, the brothers had been farmers, but once they divided their lands they ended up with nothing and had to become labourers. Shankar tried his best to avoid a division in the family but the situation was out of his control. The day they separated kitchens in their home, he cried like a baby. Brothers became enemies. All relations were broken. For several days he could not eat. He would work hard in the summer sun all day long. At night he would cover his face and go to sleep. He worked so vigorously and gave such extreme suffering to his body that he fell ill. For months he could not get up from his bed. How was he to live and on what? Between them, the brothers had five bighas of land. Now, there were just two and a half bighas and one bullock. What gain was of that? Things became so bad that he was reduced to being a farmer in name only; it was not farming that made his livelihood but working as a labourer for whoever was ready to pay him his wages.

One day, as Shankar was returning home, the priest stopped him, saying, 'Come over tomorrow and clear your accounts. You have an outstanding amount of five and a half maan[37] of wheat against you and you are showing no gesture of paying it back. You seem to have forgotten all about it!'

Stunned, Shankar asked, 'When did I take wheat from you? And how has it become five and a half maan? You seem to have forgotten: I never take so much as an ounce from anyone, nor keep a paisa of dues.'

'It is because of your greed that you are in such a poor state today,' the priest said and then mentioned the one-and-a-quarter ser of wheat Shankar had borrowed from him seven years ago. Shankar was surprised. 'Oh, my god!' he said to himself. 'I have given him a portion from my harvest

---

37. 1 maan is 40 ser.

countless times, and what has he ever done for me? Whenever he has come at my door on any occasion—good or bad—I have always given him a token sum of money. But look at his hunger! He has been sitting on that one-and-a-quarter ser of wheat like a hen sits on an egg and today it has become a spook that wants to demolish me up! Had he even hinted it in all these years, I would have measured exactly one and a quarter ser of wheat and given it to him. Was it for this day that he kept quiet for all these years?'

To the priest, he said, 'I may not have specified that I was returning the wheat I took from you but several times when you came to take your share of the produce, I would give you extra—sometimes one ser, sometimes two. Now you are asking for five and a half maan; where am I to get that?'

The priest answered, 'You can give away whatever you might please; that is extra. But you must pay up what is written in the account book; that is fixed. There is no description of what you have given. You say you gave four times the share of the harvest; maybe you did. But in my account book, there is a sum of five and a half maan of wheat written against your name. You get whomever you want to look at it and check the calculation. I will cross your name the day you settle your balance; or else the amount will keep increasing.'

Shankar answered, 'Why are you bothering a poor man like me? I have scarcely enough to eat; where will I get so much wheat from?'

'That's for you to decide. I will not forgive even one ounce. If you don't pay in this world, I shall take it from you in the other world.'

Shankar trembled with fear. An educated man like me would have said, 'Great, take it in the other world, the calculations of weight won't be more there.' But Shankar was not a clever, argumentative kind of person. A debt was unfortunate enough, but owing it to a brahmin . . . ! 'If my name remains in a brahmin's account book, I shall go straight to hell!' the very thought frightened him. He said, 'I will give whatever I owe you in this world itself; why should I wait for the other world? This birth is unpleasant enough, why should I sow thorns for my next life too? But I must say, this is not just. You have made a mountain out of a molehill. You are a brahmin; you shouldn't do such acts. You should have taken it then, not waited for it to become such an enormous amount. I shall give you whatever you will say, but you will have to answer for it before god.'

The priest answered, 'You should be afraid of facing god, I have no reason to. When I go to face god, I shall be among my brothers. Hermits, ascetics, gods—they are all brahmins. If something goes against me, we shall take care of it. So, tell me, when are you going to settle up?'

'I don't exactly have it lying at home. I can give it only after I have borrowed it from someone.'

'That does not seem right to me. It has been seven years already. I can't give you another day extra. If you can't return the wheat, sign these papers.'

'I have to return what I owe; it matters very little to me whether you take the wheat or the papers. What is the amount you will charge for the wheat?'

'The same as the market price. Instead of the five and a half maan, I shall charge you only for five and a quarter.'

'Why leave the quarter? I don't want to owe you anything and be held countable in my next life.'

When the amount was calculated, it worked out to sixty rupees. A document was prepared for sixty rupees, with interest at three rupees. If Shankar didn't pay up in a year, the interest amount would mount to two and a half rupees extra. The stamp cost, eight annas. Shankar had to bear for drawing up and writing the document.

The whole village criticized the priest, but no one could say it face to face. Everyone needed something from a moneylender. No one wanted to get into any conflict with him.

3

Shankar worked hard for a year. He had pledged himself that he would pay the sum prior to its due date. Before, food was cooked in his home only in the evening; during the day the family would survive on parched gram. In the past year, that too had come to an end. Chapatti was now made in the evenings for the little boy. The only money Shankar used to earlier spend on himself was a paisa's worth of tobacco every day. When he took his oath, he stopped that bad habit too. He tossed away his pipe, burst his hukkah and shattered the tobacco container into little pieces. His clothes were already quite tattered; now they seemed to have disappeared from sight altogether. He would spend the bitterest cold winter nights sitting beside the fire. The result of this extreme self-control was beyond his assumptions. By the end of the year, he had collected sixty rupees. He thought he would give the money to the priest and tell him he would get the rest as soon as possible. After all, it was only a matter of another fifteen rupees. Wouldn't he, after all, agree to even that? He took the sixty rupees and put them at the priest's feet. Panditji asked in surprise, 'Have you stolen them from someone?'

Shankar replied, 'No, my lord. Because of your blessings, I have been able to earn good stipends this year.'

'But these are only sixty rupees here.'

'Take this now; I will return the rest in the next two or three months and then you can set me free.'

'I shall set you free only when you have returned every last penny that you owe me. Go and get the fifteen rupees that you still owe me.'

'Have mercy on me; I stay hungry all day, in the evenings too sometimes I get to eat, sometimes I don't. I live in this village. I am not going to run away with your money.'

'I don't want to get into the trouble of tracking you. If I don't get all my money back, I shall start charging interest at the rate of three and a half rupees. You can take your sixty rupees back with you, or you can leave them with me.'

'All right; keep the money. I'll go and try to organize fifteen rupees from somewhere.'

Shankar tried his best but no one gave him the money— not because people didn't trust him or they didn't have the money to give, but because no one had the fearlessness to take away the priest's easy prey.

4

Every action has a reaction. Despite working so hard for an entire year, Shankar could still not free himself from debt, his determination turned naturally into distress. He understood that if his year-long hardships could fetch him not more than sixty rupees, there was no way that he could possibly save twice as much in the coming year. If he must sway under the burden of debt, it mattered little whether the load on his head weighed one maan or a maan and a quarter.

His enthusiasm to repay the debt minimised. He began to hate hard work.

Hope is the mother of passion. Hope has strength and power. It is the only energy that drives the world. Shankar became hopeless and, therefore, depressed. Those needs that he had kept at bay for the past year were no longer like beggars who came and stood at his door; they turned into evil spirits that sit on your chest and deny to go away till they have got what they want from you. There is a limit to the patches you can put on your clothes. Now when Shankar got his wages, he would not save a single rupee. Sometimes he would buy clothes, at other times get something to eat. Where earlier he used to only smoke tobacco, now he picked up the bad habit of smoking. He was in no hurry to repay the loan. He acted as though he didn't owe anyone a single paisa. Earlier he would go to work even when he had a fever; now he looked for excuses not to work.

Three years passed in this manner. The priest didn't come for his money even once. Like a clever trapper, he waited for the right occasion to trap. It was against his policy to alert the prey to the danger lying in rest.

One day, the priest sent for Shankar and showed him the accounts. After deducting the sixty rupees already deposited, there were still 120 rupees owing against Shankar's name.

Shankar said, 'I can give you that amount of money in some other birth, not in this one!'

'But I shall take it in this very lifetime. If you can't return the capital, you must at least pay the interest.'

'I have nothing except one bullock; take that if you want.'

'What will I do with your bullock? You still have a lot to give me.'

'What else is there?'

'You are there. After all, you go somewhere to work, don't you, and I too have to keep someone to care for my lands. You start working for me to pay off your interest and return the capital whenever you can. The truth is that now you can no longer work for anyone else till you return all the money you owe me. No one would be willing to employ you, knowing that you owe me money. You have no property, nothing that you can keep with me instead of the money you owe me. So how can I let you off? Is there anyone to ensure that you will pay my interest amount every month? When you can't work anywhere else to return the interest amount, it cannot be imagined that you will ever return the capital.'

'If I work for you to repay the interest, how shall I live on?'

'You have a wife and children; have they had their hands chopped off that they must sit leisurely at home? Let them work too. I shall give you half a ser of barley to eat every day. Once a year I shall give you a blanket and also get a quilted jacket stitched for you to keep you warm. What else do you need? While it is true that others paid you six annas, I don't really need you that much. I am employing you only to help you repay your loan.'

Shankar was lost in deep thought. Then he said, 'This sounds like life-long slavery.'

'You can call it slavery, or you can call it salary. But I am not going to leave you till you return the money you owe me. If you run away, your son will have to return it. Though if no one remains from your family, it will be a different matter then.'

There was no appeal against such a declaration. Who would come forward to help a labourer? There was nowhere to take shelter or run to. Shankar began to work for the priest starting the next day. For the sake of one-and-a-quarter ser of wheat, he had to wear the chains of slavery for the rest of his life. If there was anything to give him sympathy it was the thought that he was being penalized for a previous birth. His wife had to do tasks she had never done before. His children were nearly always starving. And Shankar could do nothing except quietly watch them suffer. Like a curse of the gods, those grains of wheat were never to leave his life.

5

Shankar worked for the priest as an unpaid slave for twenty long years till he left this world that had treated him so badly. At the time of his death, a sum of 120 rupees was still written against his name. The priest didn't consider it suitable to bother him in the other world; after all, he wasn't such a cruel man! Instead, he caught hold of Shankar's son. The young man still works for the priest. When he will be set free, whether he will be set free or not—God alone has the answer.

12. The Gift of Truth

Munshi Bhavani Sahay, the headmaster of the tehsil school of Baranv, was excessively fond of gardening. He had planted different kinds of leaves and flowers, rows upon rows, in the small school garden. Creepers embellished doors. The beauty of the school had indeed doubled. He would also regularly take the help of his middle school students to care for and water the plants and clean up his garden. Most of the boys would work happily. It would keep them occupied. However, there was a group which included four to five boys from the zamindar community. They possessed a certain vicious characteristic which forced them to regard such fruitful work as unpaid labour. These boys had lived a lazy life since childhood. Their hearts were filled with the arrogance that wealth brings. Physical labour was beneath their dignity. They hated the garden. When it was their turn to do the work, they would make some excuse or the other and disappear from the scene. They would in fact create further damage by instigating their classmates with taunts such as, 'Wonderful! Learn Persian to become an oil vendor. Why hit our heads against books if we have to work with spades . . . We come here to study, not to work as labourers.' Mr. Munshi would sometimes punish them for their impertinence. This would fan their disinclination further. Finally, one day, matters came to such a point that these boys decided to destroy the flower garden. The school began at ten, but that morning they arrived by eight and began to uproot the plants bit by bit. Here the plants were ruthlessly pulled out, there the beds mercilessly trodded upon, water pipes broken, and the raised edges of the flower beds dug up. Their hearts beat wildly in their chests with the fear of being noticed. But how long does it take to destroy a tiny garden patch? In ten minutes the verdant little square looked war-torn and shattered. The boys ran out in a rush. At the gate, however, they noticed a classmate of theirs—Baz Bahadur, a lean and poor but intelligent boy. He was considerate and silent. As it was, these unrestrained fellows grudged him. Now their blood went cold. They realised that he would have seen what they had been up to. He would surely report them to Mr. Munshi. Bad luck, what a terrible beginning! But what was the rascal up to here at this hour? The boys exchanged meaningful looks. Everyone was of the opinion that he should be made part of their group. Jagat Singh was the leader. He moved forward to call out. 'Baz Bahadur, how come you are here untimely? Today, we have freed your neck from the noose around it. Masterji[38] would bother us too much, do this, do that. But remember: do not spill the beans on us because he will really make us pay for this.'

Jayaram put into words, 'What will he say, he is now with us. We've done this for everyone, not for ourselves alone. Come, friend, let's walk to the bazaar together and have some sweets.'

Baz Bahadur replied, 'No, I didn't find time at home today to learn my lessons. I'd rather sit here and study.'

Jagat Singh said, 'Fine, but you won't say anything to Mr. Munshi, right?'

---

38. Addressing teacher with respect.

'I won't say anything on my own, but what if he asks me?'

'Just say that you know nothing about it.'

'I will not tell a lie.'

Jayaram warned, 'If you gossip about us and we get punished for it, we will beat you to death.'

Baz Bahadur said, 'I've already told you. I won't complain to Mr. Munshi but neither will I lie to him about it.'

'Then we will break your bones for it.'

'Yes, you have the right to do so.'

At ten when school started and Munshi Bhavani Sahay noticed his ruined garden, he lost his temper. He was not half as upset at the state his garden was in as much as at the way the boys had acted. Had a bull inflicted this destruction, he would have only repented the matter. But he would never tolerate such a fit of anger by his students. As soon as the boys sat down in class, he walked in and thundered, 'Who is responsible for the state of the garden?'

The classroom turned quiet. The guilty boys felt their faces drained of colour. Not one of the twenty-five middle school students was unaware of what went on earlier that morning. But not one was courageous enough to stand up and claim knowledge of it. Each one of them sat silent, head down. Mr. Munshi's temper flared further at this scene. He shouted again, 'I am certain it is one amongst you. Those who know of it can tell me honestly. Or else, I will begin to cane you all in a row. Then none of you will be able to say that you were innocent.'

But not one boy uttered a word. The silence continued.

Mr. Munshi asked, 'Devi Prasad, do you know anything?'

'No Masterji, I don't know anything about it.'

'Shivdas, what about you?'

'No, Masterji, I know nothing.'

'Baz Bahadur, you never tell a lie. Are you aware of anything?'

Baz Bahadur stood up, his face permeated with the glow of heroism. His eyes shone with courage. He spoke up, 'Yes, Masterji.'

Mr. Munshi said, 'Wonderful, very good! Well done!'

The culprits glared at Baz Bahadur, their eyes filled with hatred. And thought, fine, so be it!

Bhavani Sahay was an infinitely patient human being. As long as he could, he did not torture his students. But he would not feel even a pinch of repentance to punish such wickedness. He caned each of the culprits five times, kept them standing on the bench throughout the day and put the dreaded black cross against their names in the conduct register.

As it was, the mischief-making group had always been jealous of Baz Bahadur. However, now his honesty had made them thirsty for his blood. Suffering births sympathy. So, at this moment, most of the class sympathized and sided with the culprits. And they all began to plot how to teach Baz Bahadur a lesson. Break his bones; he should not be able to come back to school again. A traitor amongst friends! Such betrayal. Honest Jack indeed. Today, he will pay the price for his honesty. Poor Baz Bahadur was completely unaware of the conspiracy being planned behind his back. His classmates took every precaution to keep him in the dark.

Baz Bahadur began walking home after school. There was a guava orchard along the way. Jayaram and Jagat Singh waited there with the others. Baz Bahadur saw them and was taken aback. He understood that his classmates were determined to punish him and that there really was no way to escape them. He moved forward, fearful. Jagat Singh spoke up, 'Come, my dear. You've kept us waiting long. Come, and accept our award for your honesty.'

Baz Bahadur said, 'Move off, let me go.'

Jayaram taunted him, 'Come on, at least taste the fruits of truthfulness.'

Baz Bahadur replied, 'Look, I had warned you that I would tell him if he would ask me directly.'

'Well, we had also warned you that we will not let you off without suitably rewarding you for your efforts.'

Having said that Jayaram moved towards Baz Bahadur, and aimed a punch towards him. Jagat Singh tried to hold both his arms. Shivram, Jayaram's younger brother, leapt at him armed with a guava branch. The rest of the boys stood around, spectators to the game. They were the 'reserve' soldiers, ready to pounce into the commotion to defend their friends.

Baz Bahadur was a weak boy. His three hefty opponents were enough to take care of him. The boys were ready to see him lose in a few moments. Baz Bahadur realized that his enemies had begun their well-planned attack. He darted a few glances this way and that, grabbed Shivram's guava branch from him and stepped back a few inches. Flaunting the branch like a sword, he said, 'Who are you all to punish or reward me for my honesty?'

Both sides made moves and countermoves. Baz Bahadur may have been weak but he was neither slow nor absent-minded. And to add to that, his confidence in his stand gave him firmness. No matter if he was executed for his honesty, he would not withdraw from this battle. For several minutes Baz Bahadur continued to skip around and push back his opponents. But for how long could a tiny guava branch hold back the boys? In a while, it was broken. As long as Baz Bahadur had held it in his hands it had been a sword. No one dared to come close to him. And once empty-handed, he had tried to fight back by kicking and punching the others. But in the end, the majority won. Shivram threw such a tremendous punch in his ribs that Baz Bahadur fell down, wheezing for breath. His eyes closed. When his enemies saw his condition, they were at a loss for what to do. Thinking him dead, they disappeared slowly.

After about ten minutes, Baz Bahadur regained consciousness. His chest hurt. The blow had been successful. Moreover, he had no strength to stand up. He showed courage and rose to make his way home.

Meanwhile, the victory party arrived at Jayaram's house. The rest of the class had dispersed along the way. Some ran this way, others that; it was a thankless situation. Only three steadfast warriors reached Jayaram's house. Once they had entered the gates, they could breathe again.

Jayaram: 'I hope he's not dead. My punch was bad.'

Jagat Singh: 'You should not have aimed at his ribs. If you punctured his spleen, he won't survive.'

Jayaram: 'Come on, I didn't do that intentionally. It was just an accident. What should we do now?'

Jagat: 'Just sit tight.'

Jayaram: 'I hope I alone don't get caught for it.'

Jagat: 'We are all in it together.'

Jayaram: 'If Baz Bahadur isn't dead, the first thing he'll surely do is head to Mr. Munshi.'

Jagat: 'And then Mr. Munshi will most certainly condemn us alive.'

Jayaram: 'That is why I feel we should not go to school tomorrow. Let's enrol in another school. Or else, be unwell for some time. In a month or two, the matter will be forgotten and then we can take a decision.'

Shivram: 'And what about the forthcoming exams?'

Jayaram: 'Oh no, I had completely forgotten about them. We only have a month to go.'

Jagat: 'This time you would have got a scholarship.'

Jayaram: 'Yes, I have really worked hard for it. So?'

Jagat: 'Well, you may not manage the scholarship, though you may get promoted.'

Jayaram: 'Baz Bahadur will get it.'

Jagat: 'Good for him. Poor guy has really taken a thrashing from us.'

The next day school began as usual. Jagat Singh, Jayaram and Shivram were missing. Wali Mohammad came but with his foot bandaged. He was all scared. The previous day's spectators sat silently with their hearts in their mouths, hoping to not be thrashed with the culprits. Baz Bahadur was busy with his work as usual. It seemed as if he had forgotten fully about the incident that had happened the day before. No one discussed the topic either. Of course, he did seem jollier than his usual self. In fact, he was friendlier with the ones who were his opponents yesterday. He really wanted to assure the boys that he bore no misgivings about them. He had come to this point after having thought hard about it all night. And by the time he was going back home from school, he had received the fruit of his kindness. His enemies were shamefaced and he was praised by all.

However, the three main culprits of the crime did not come to school the next day. Even on the third day, they did not turn up. They would leave home for school but turn to the fields instead. They would roam around under some tree or the other or spend time playing gulli-danda. In the evening they would get back home.

They had, for sure come to know, that the other soldiers of their battle were going to school and that Mr. Munshi had not said anything to them. However, it was extremely hard to hush the suspicion that resided within them. Baz Bahadur must have complained about them surely. They only had to go back to school and they wouldn't be left to live. This thought would not allow them to return to school.

Early morning on the fourth day after the incident, the boys sat around pondering which way they should go. They suddenly saw Baz Bahadur coming their way. Though they were astonished to see him, they also felt a sense of relief. Baz Bahadur began even before they could open their mouths. 'Why friends, why aren't you attending school? You have been absent for three days now.'

Jagat: 'How can we go to school? We're scared out of our own shrewdness. Mr. Munshi will not spare a single bone in our bodies.'

Baz Bahadur: 'Why so? Wali Mohammad, Durga, each one of them has been coming. Mr. Munshi has not said a word to them.'

Jayaram: 'You may have left those boys but why would you do the same for us? You must, in fact, have tripled your complaints against us.'

Baz Bahadur: 'Why don't you come to school and check if this is true?'

Jagat: 'Stop trying to fool us. This must be a plan to get us punished.'

Baz Bahadur: 'I am not running away, am I? You rewarded me for my honesty the other day, now you can reward me for telling a lie.'

Jayaram: 'You really haven't complained about us?'

Baz Bahadur: 'What was there to complain about? You hit me and I hit you back. If you had not punched me that day, I would have forced you off the battlefield. I am not in the habit of gossiping about fights amongst us.'

Jagat: 'I still can't trust you. If you lie to us, you'll be beaten to a pulp again.'

Baz Bahadur: 'You know I don't tell lies.' He spoke in such a manner that the boys were assured about what he was saying. After he left they remained deep in conversation about what had just come to light. At last, they decided to risk going to school.

At exactly ten, they arrived at school, still very fearful, their faces drained of colour.

Mr. Munshi walked into the room. The boys stood up to welcome him. He glared at the three boys sharply but all he said was, 'You have been absent for three days now. Make sure you copy the notes for the days you have missed.' Then he became occupied in the lessons.

When it was time for the half-hour water break, the three boys and some others clustered together to chat.

Jayaram: 'Well, we took a huge risk in returning to school but Baz Bahadur was indeed true to his word.'

Wali Mohammad: 'I am convinced that he is not a human but a God. Had I not been a witness to all that has happened I would never have believed any of it.'

Jagat: 'He truly is goodness exemplified. We have committed a grave mistake by meting out such injustice to him.'

Durga: 'Let's go ask for his forgiveness.'

Jayaram: 'What a wonderful idea. Let's do it right now.'

When school ended for the day, the entire class went to Baz Bahadur. Jagat Singh again assumed leadership of the group. He spoke up, 'Brother! We have all misjudged you. We are extremely ashamed for having made you suffer. Do forgive our crime. You are a model of virtue whereas we are uncultured, illiterate and stupid. Do forgive us.'

Baz Bahadur's eyes filled with tears. He replied, 'I have always thought of you all as my brothers, and I still do. What is there to forgive between brothers?'

The boys clasped each other. The news spread throughout the school. All the students of the school began to worship Baz Bahadur. He became a leader and the head boy of the school.

Baz Bahadur was first penalised for the truth and then remunerated for it as well.

www.ingramcontent.com/pod-product-compliance
Lightning Source LLC
Chambersburg PA
CBHW020931160726

47993CB00005B/2234